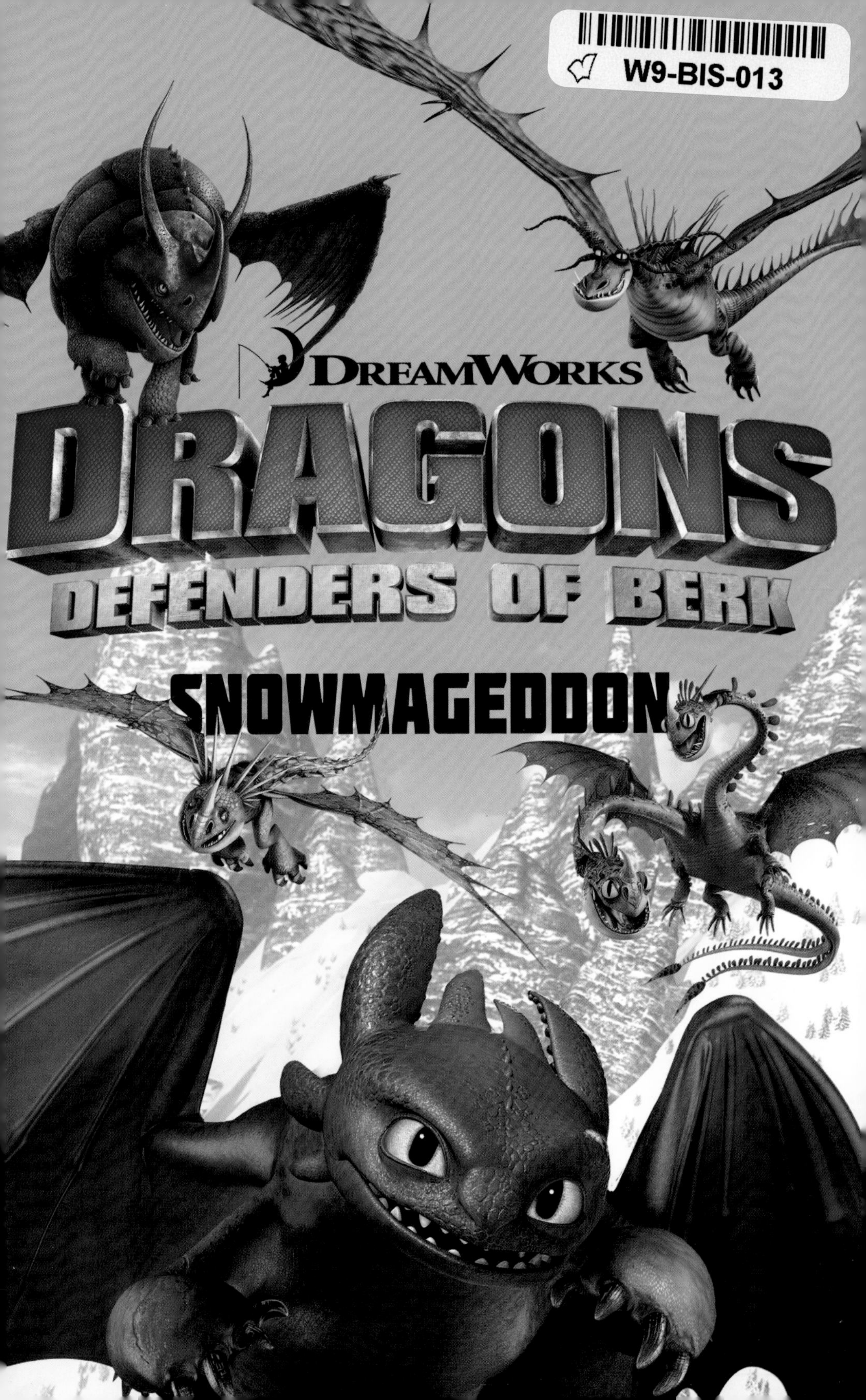
DREAMWORKS
DRAGONS
DEFENDERS OF BERK
SNOWMAGEDDON

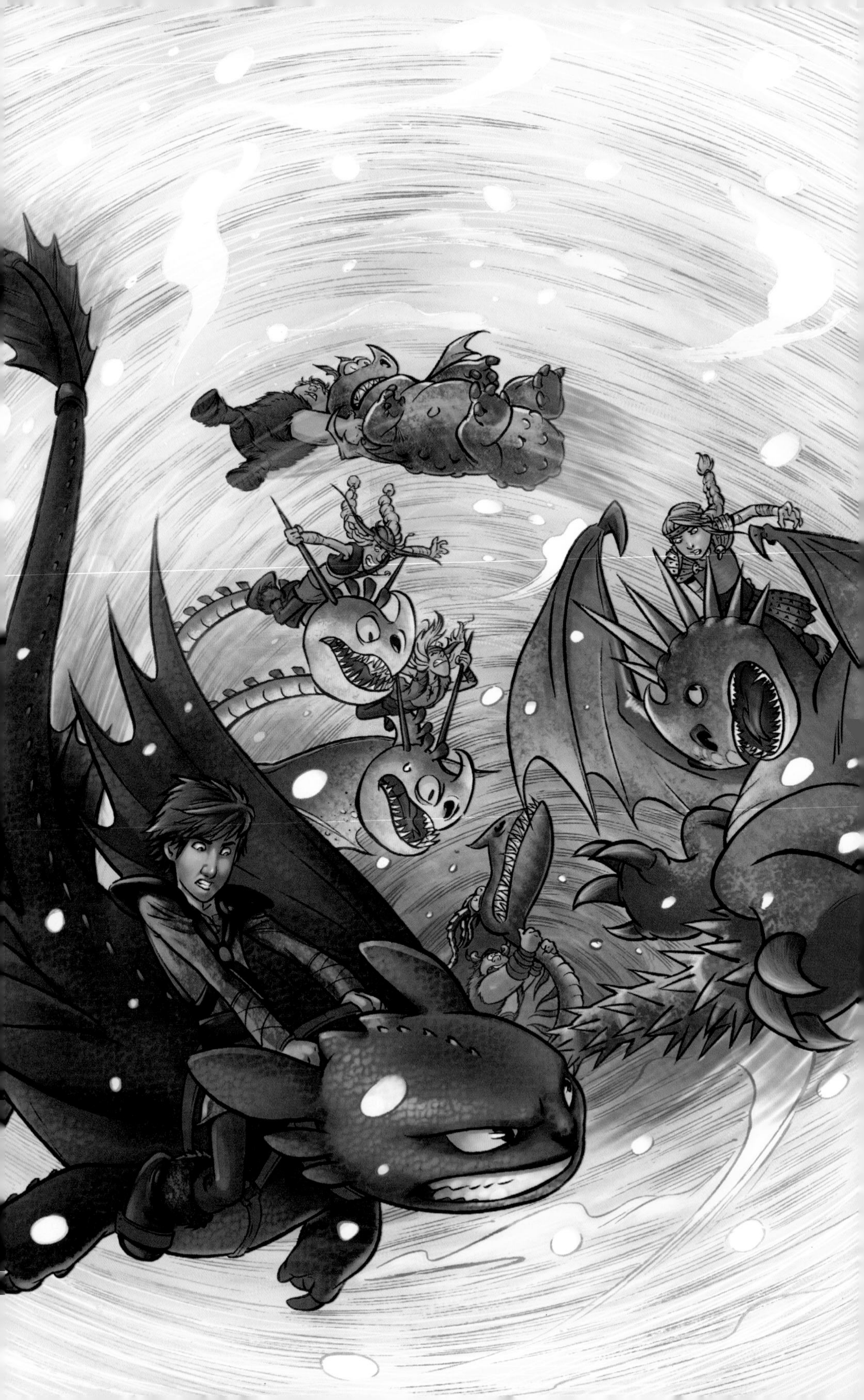

DreamWorks

DRAGONS
DEFENDERS OF BERK

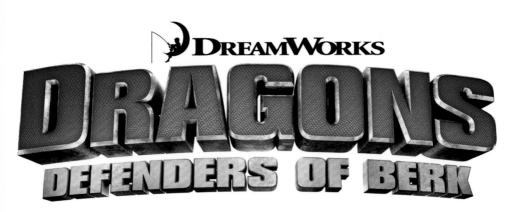

SNOWMAGEDDON

SCRIPT
SIMON FURMAN

PENCILS
IWAN NAZIF

COLORS
DIGIKORE

LETTERING
JIM CAMPBELL

PLUS: SPECIAL BONUS STORY
THAW FLEET

TITAN
COMICS

DREAMWORKS

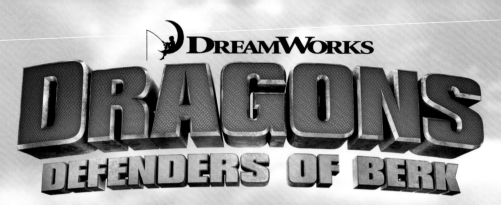

DRAGONS
DEFENDERS OF BERK

Welcome to Berk, the home of Hiccup and his dragon, Toothless, plus Hiccup's friends who train at the Dragon Training Academy!

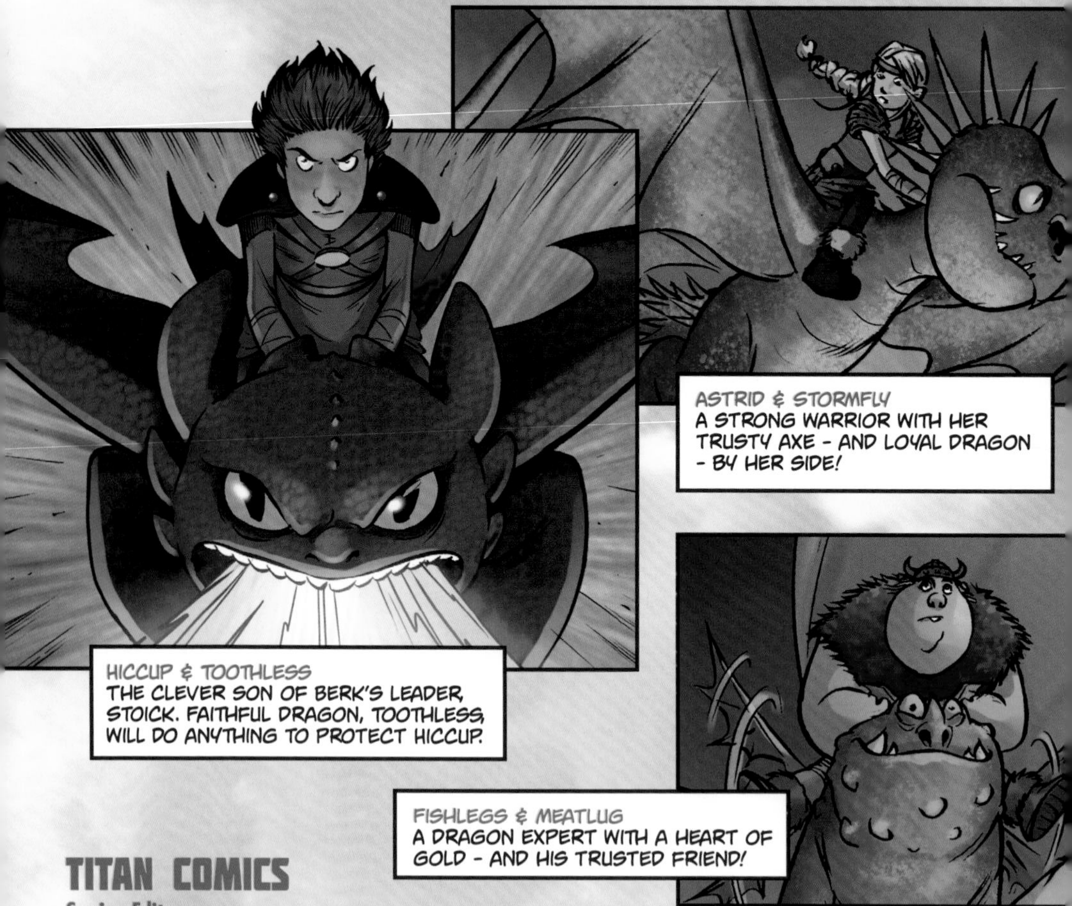
ASTRID & STORMFLY
A STRONG WARRIOR WITH HER TRUSTY AXE - AND LOYAL DRAGON - BY HER SIDE!
HICCUP & TOOTHLESS
THE CLEVER SON OF BERK'S LEADER, STOICK. FAITHFUL DRAGON, TOOTHLESS, WILL DO ANYTHING TO PROTECT HICCUP.
FISHLEGS & MEATLUG
A DRAGON EXPERT WITH A HEART OF GOLD - AND HIS TRUSTED FRIEND!

TITAN COMICS

Senior Editor
MARTIN EDEN
Production Manager
OBI ONUORA
Production Supervisors
MARIA PEARSON, JACKIE FLOOK

Production Assistant
PETER JAMES
Studio Manager
EMMA SMITH
Senior Sales Manager
STEVE TOTHILL

Marketing Manager
RICKY CLAYDON
Publishing Manager
DARRYL TOTHILL
Publishing Director
CHRIS TEATHER

Operations Director
LEIGH BAULCH
Executive Director
VIVIAN CHEUNG
Publisher
NICK LANDAU

RUFFNUT & TUFFNUT/BARF & BELCH
THESE TROUBLESOME TWINS AND THEIR TWO-HEADED DRAGON MAKE FOR A DOUBLY POWERFUL FORCE.

STOICK THE VAST
THE TOUGH CHIEF OF BERK, AND HICCUP'S DEMANDING FATHER.

GOBBER
A LONG-TIME FRIEND AND ADVISOR OF STOICK.

SNOTLOUT & HOOKFANG
SLIGHTLY RECKLESS AND STUBBORN, SNOTLOUT IS A DYNAMIC MEMBER OF THE GANG - ESPECIALLY WITH HOOKFANG BY HIS SIDE.

ISBN: 9781782762157
DreamWorks Dragons: Defenders of Berk: Snowmageddon, published by Titan Comics, a division of Titan Publishing Group Ltd.
144 Southwark St. London, SE1 0UP
10 9 8 7 6 5 4 3 2 1
First printed in China in June 2016.
A CIP catalogue record for this title is available from the British Library.
Titan Comics. TC0519
Special thanks to Corinne Combs, Barbara Layman, Lawrence Hamashima, & all at DreamWorks. Thanks to Andre Siregar at Glasshouse Graphics, and Manik Tilekar and all at Digikore.

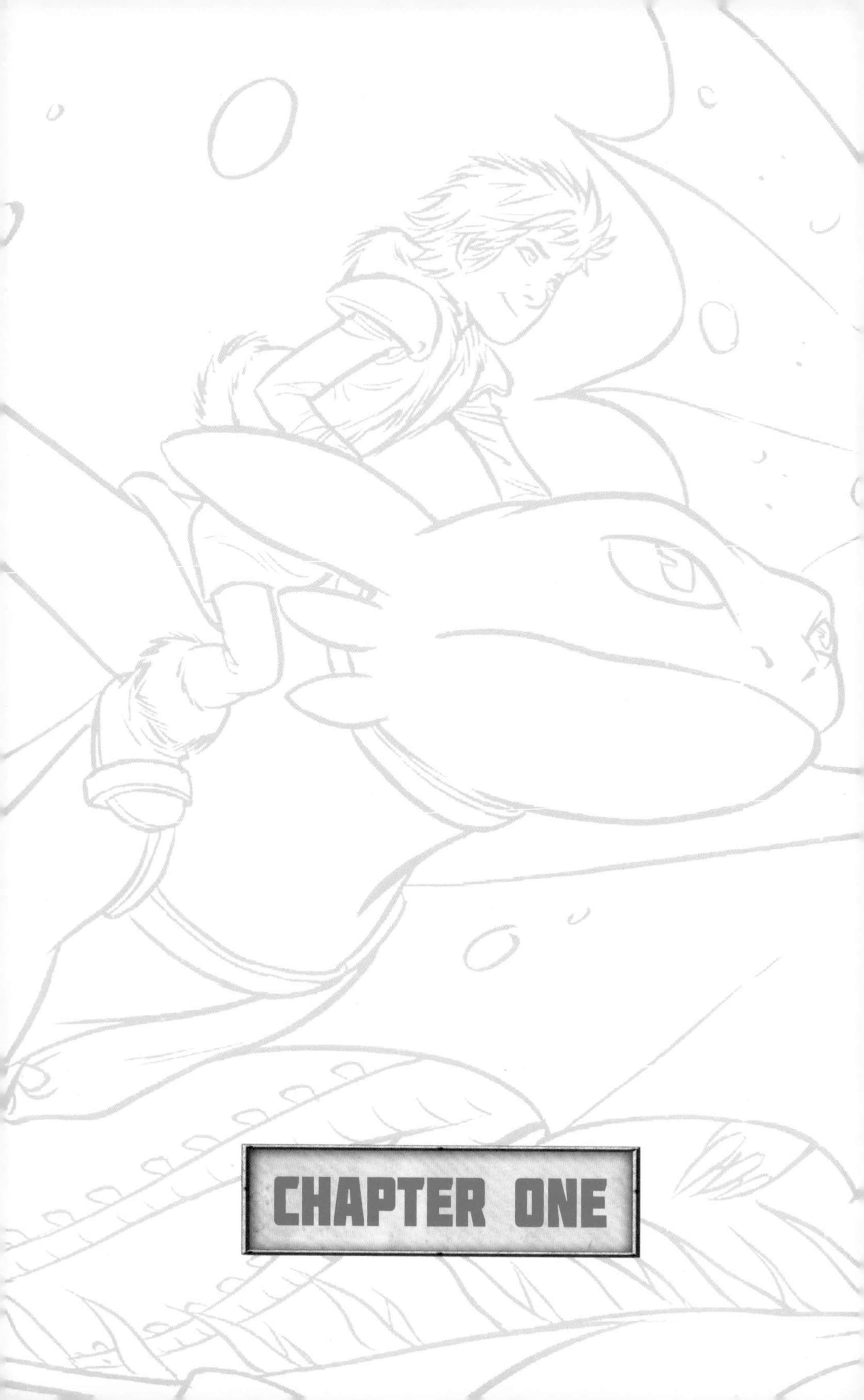

CHAPTER ONE

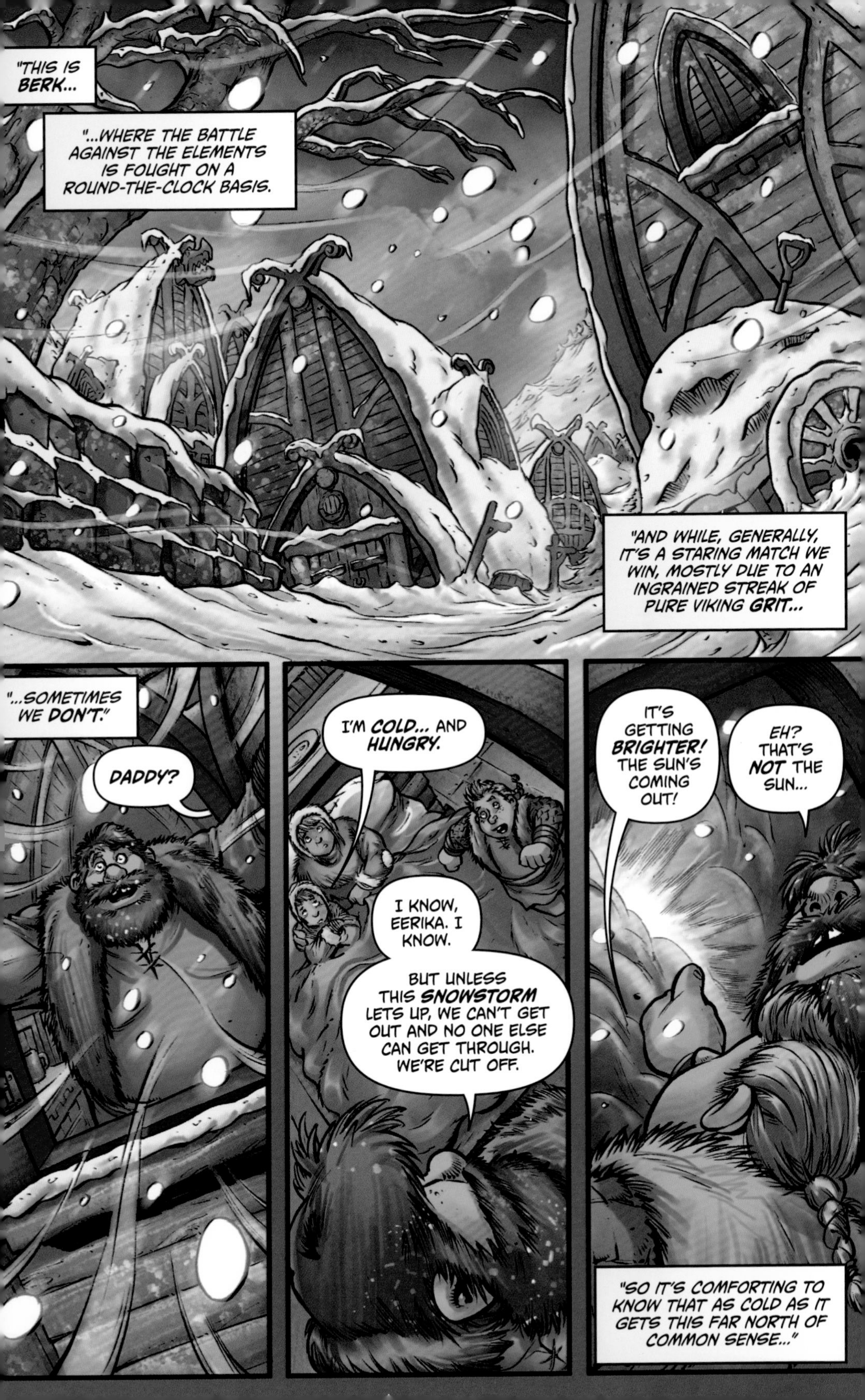
"THIS IS BERK...
"...WHERE THE BATTLE AGAINST THE ELEMENTS IS FOUGHT ON A ROUND-THE-CLOCK BASIS.
"AND WHILE, GENERALLY, IT'S A STARING MATCH WE WIN, MOSTLY DUE TO AN INGRAINED STREAK OF PURE VIKING GRIT...
"...SOMETIMES WE DON'T."
DADDY?
I'M COLD... AND HUNGRY.
I KNOW, EERIKA. I KNOW.
BUT UNLESS THIS SNOWSTORM LETS UP, WE CAN'T GET OUT AND NO ONE ELSE CAN GET THROUGH. WE'RE CUT OFF.
IT'S GETTING BRIGHTER! THE SUN'S COMING OUT!
EH? THAT'S NOT THE SUN...
"SO IT'S COMFORTING TO KNOW THAT AS COLD AS IT GETS THIS FAR NORTH OF COMMON SENSE..."

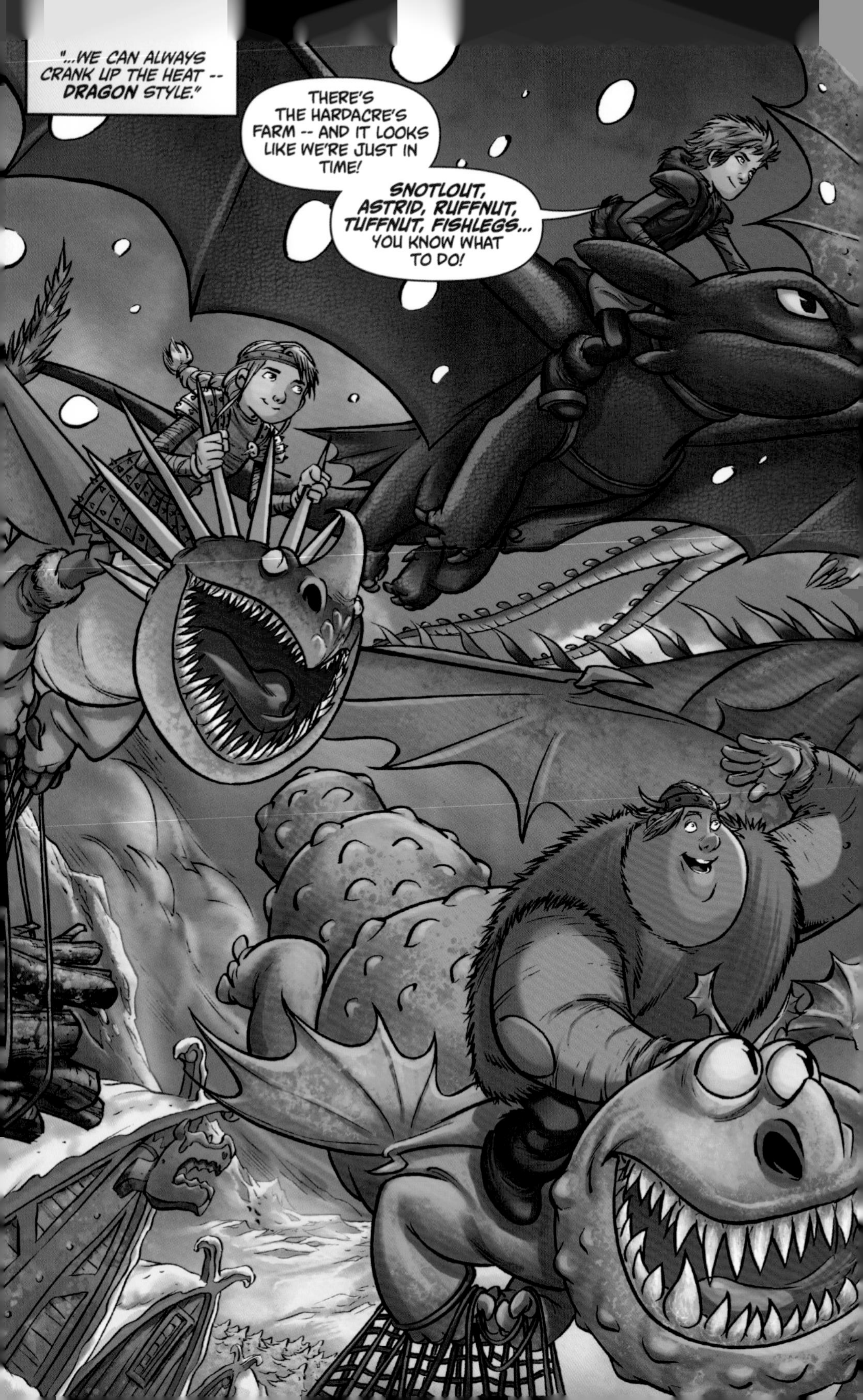
"...WE CAN ALWAYS CRANK UP THE HEAT -- DRAGON STYLE."
THERE'S THE HARDACRE'S FARM -- AND IT LOOKS LIKE WE'RE JUST IN TIME!
SNOTLOUT, ASTRID, RUFFNUT, TUFFNUT, FISHLEGS... YOU KNOW WHAT TO DO!

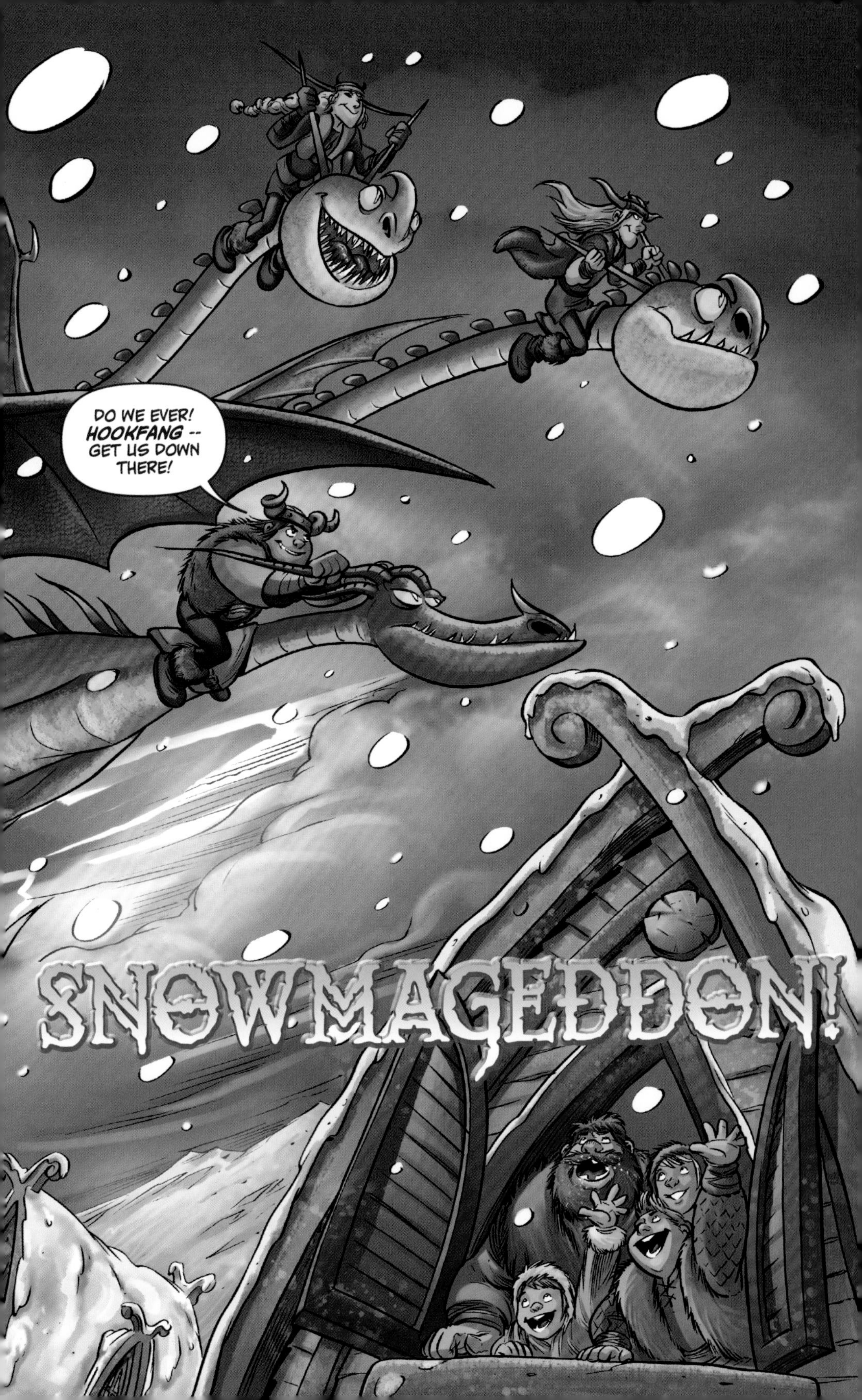
DO WE EVER! **HOOKFANG** -- GET US DOWN THERE!
SNOWMAGEDDON!

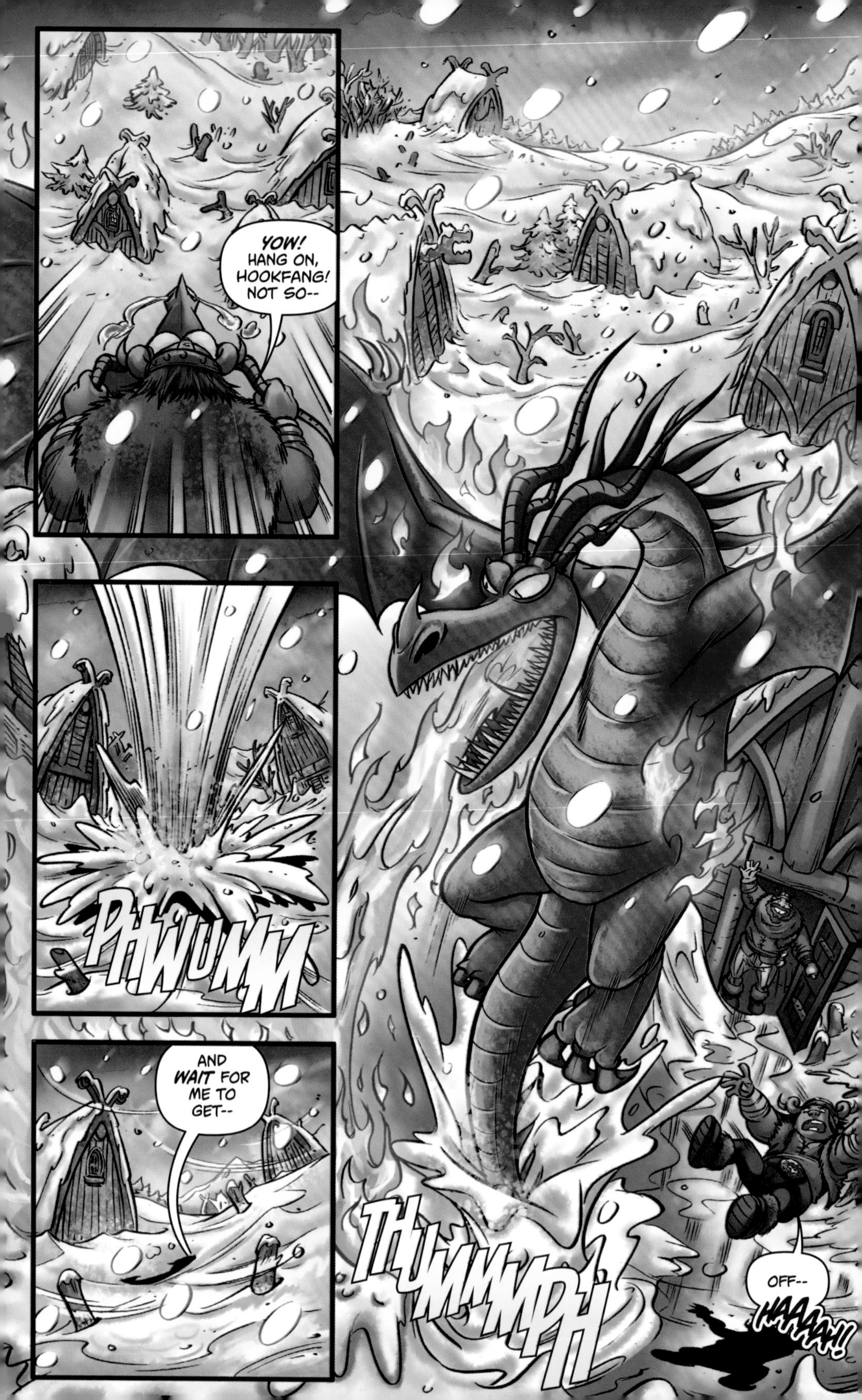
YOW! HANG ON, HOOKFANG! NOT SO--
PHWUMM
AND WAIT FOR ME TO GET--
THUMMMPH
OFF--
HAAAAH!

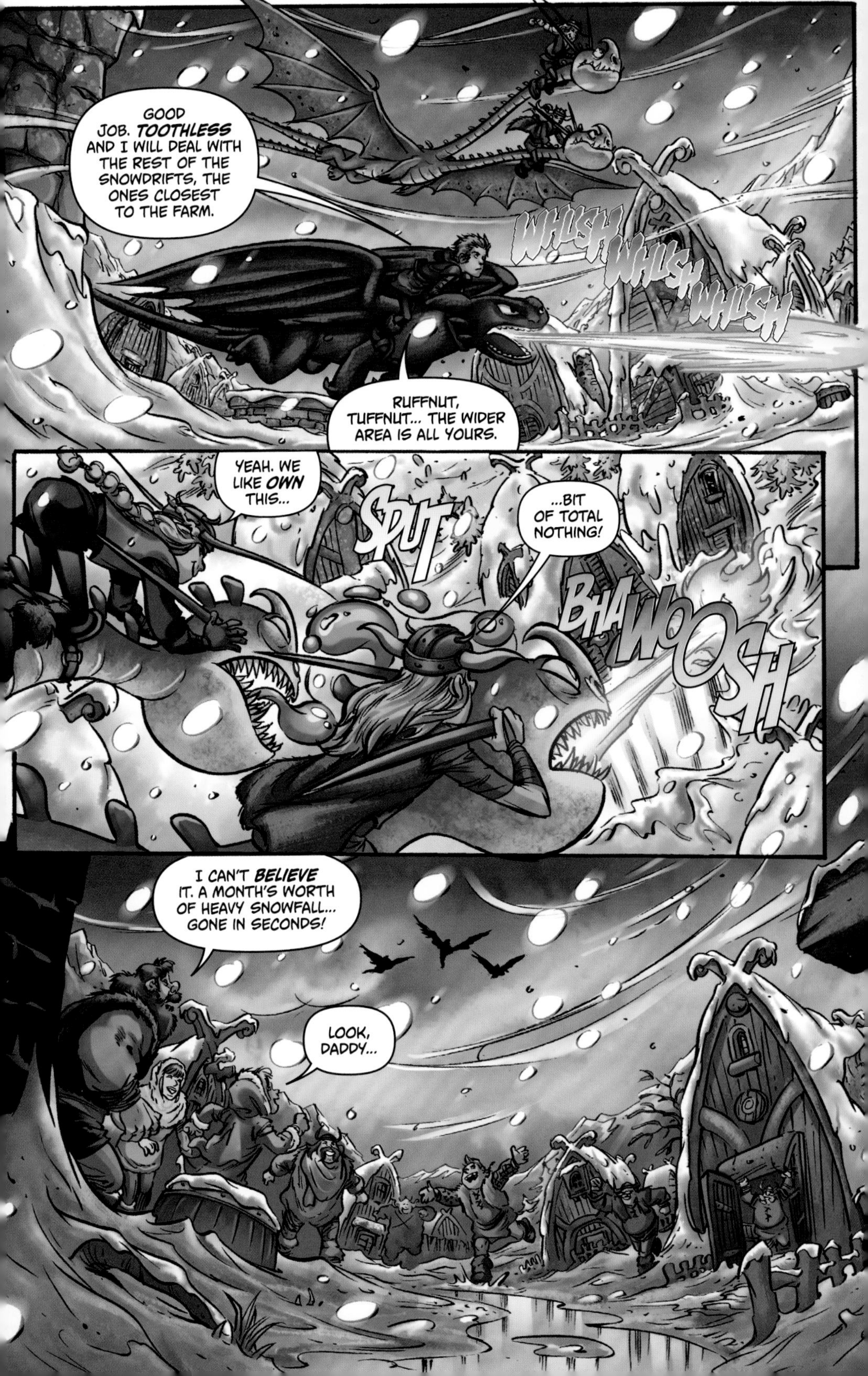
GOOD JOB. TOOTHLESS AND I WILL DEAL WITH THE REST OF THE SNOWDRIFTS, THE ONES CLOSEST TO THE FARM.
WHUSH WHUSH WHUSH
RUFFNUT, TUFFNUT... THE WIDER AREA IS ALL YOURS.
YEAH. WE LIKE OWN THIS...
SPUT
...BIT OF TOTAL NOTHING!
BHAWOOSH
I CAN'T BELIEVE IT. A MONTH'S WORTH OF HEAVY SNOWFALL... GONE IN SECONDS!
LOOK, DADDY...

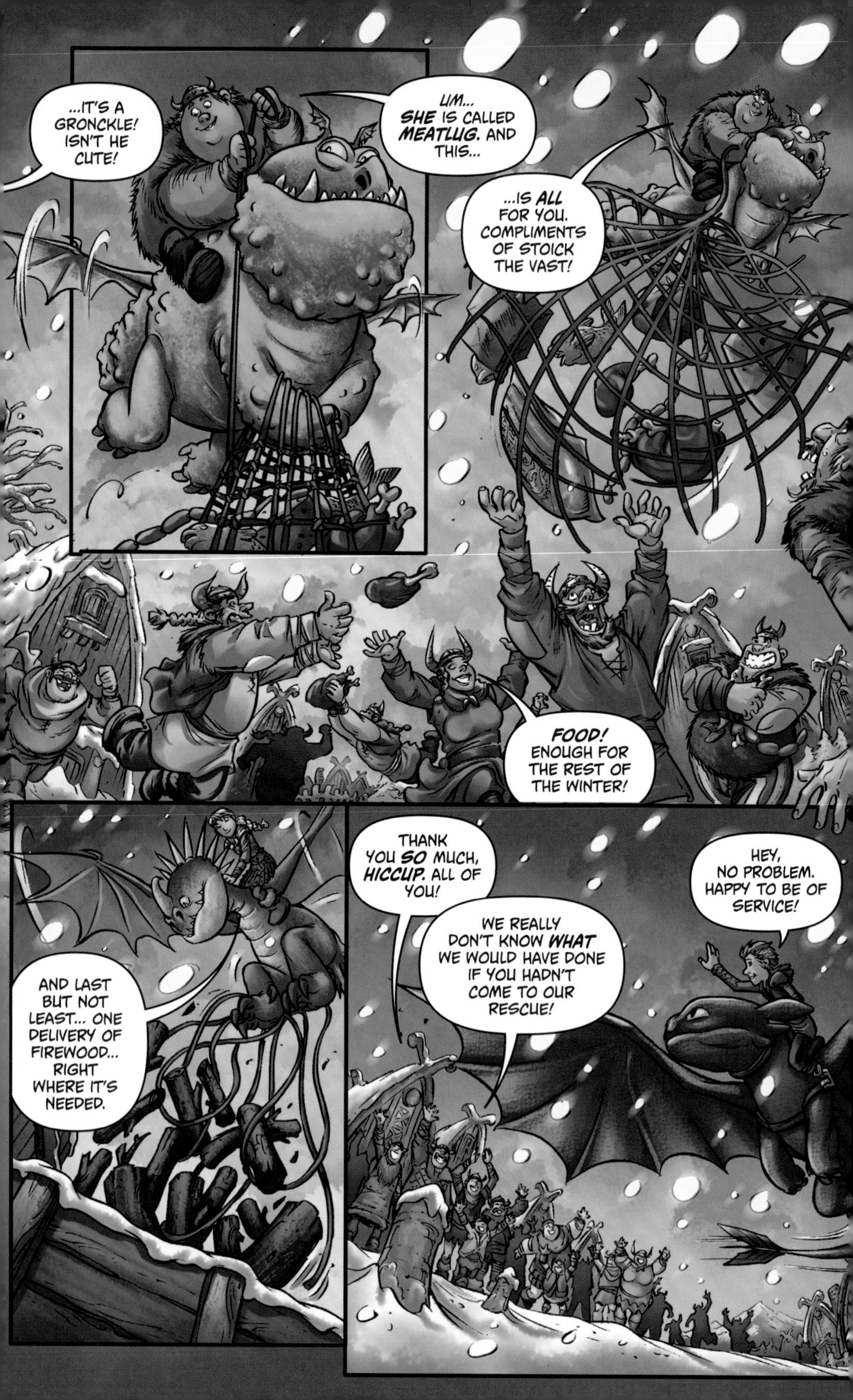
...IT'S A GRONCKLE! ISN'T HE CUTE!
UM... SHE IS CALLED MEATLUG. AND THIS...
...IS ALL FOR YOU. COMPLIMENTS OF STOICK THE VAST!
FOOD! ENOUGH FOR THE REST OF THE WINTER!
AND LAST BUT NOT LEAST... ONE DELIVERY OF FIREWOOD... RIGHT WHERE IT'S NEEDED.
THANK YOU SO MUCH, HICCUP. ALL OF YOU!
WE REALLY DON'T KNOW WHAT WE WOULD HAVE DONE IF YOU HADN'T COME TO OUR RESCUE!
HEY, NO PROBLEM. HAPPY TO BE OF SERVICE!

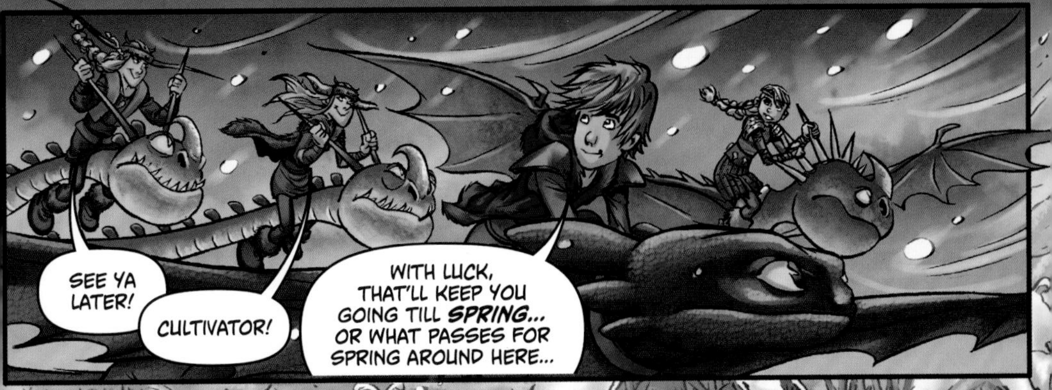
SEE YA LATER!
CULTIVATOR!
WITH LUCK, THAT'LL KEEP YOU GOING TILL SPRING... OR WHAT PASSES FOR SPRING AROUND HERE...

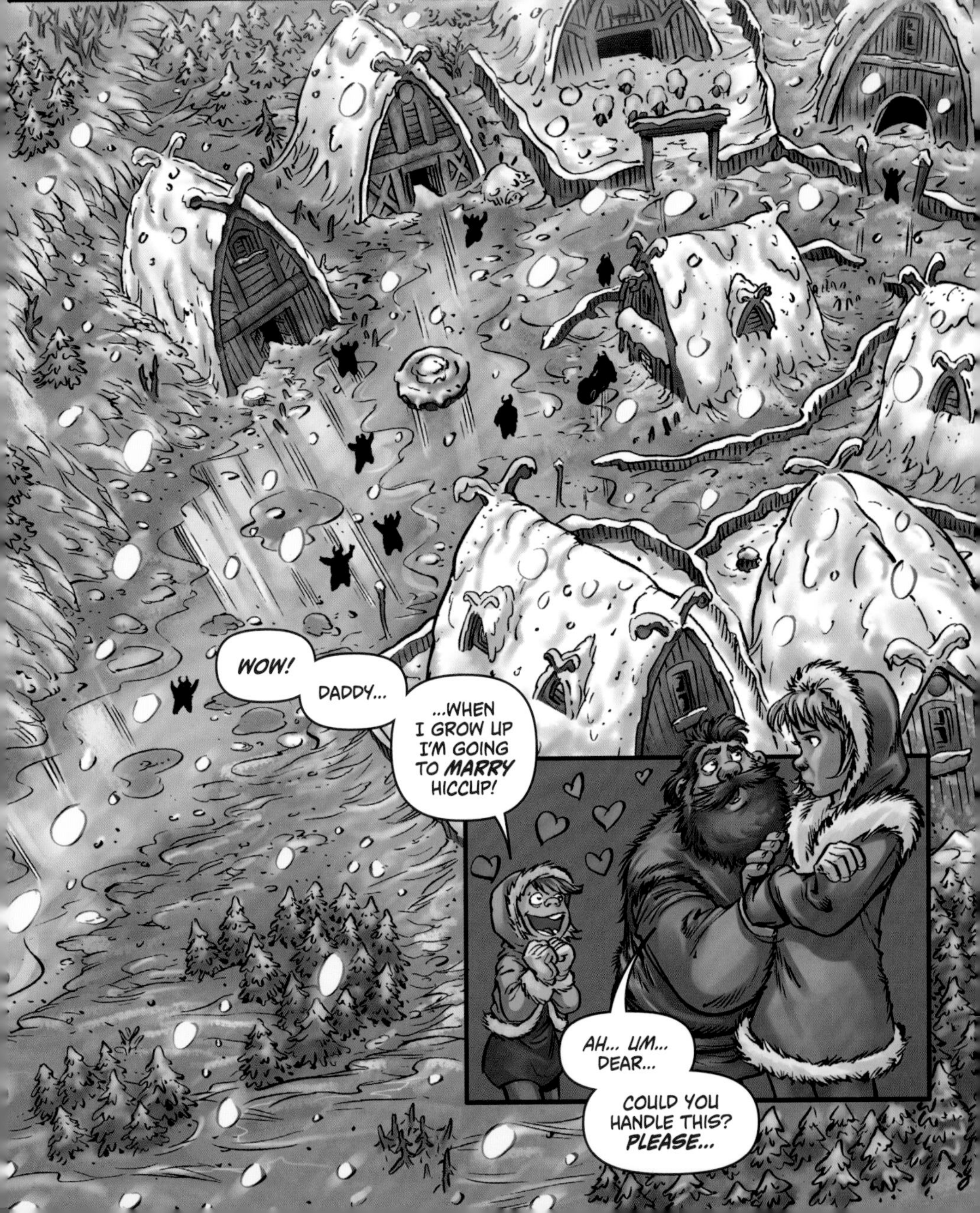
WOW!
DADDY...
...WHEN I GROW UP I'M GOING TO MARRY HICCUP!
AH... UM... DEAR...
COULD YOU HANDLE THIS? PLEASE...

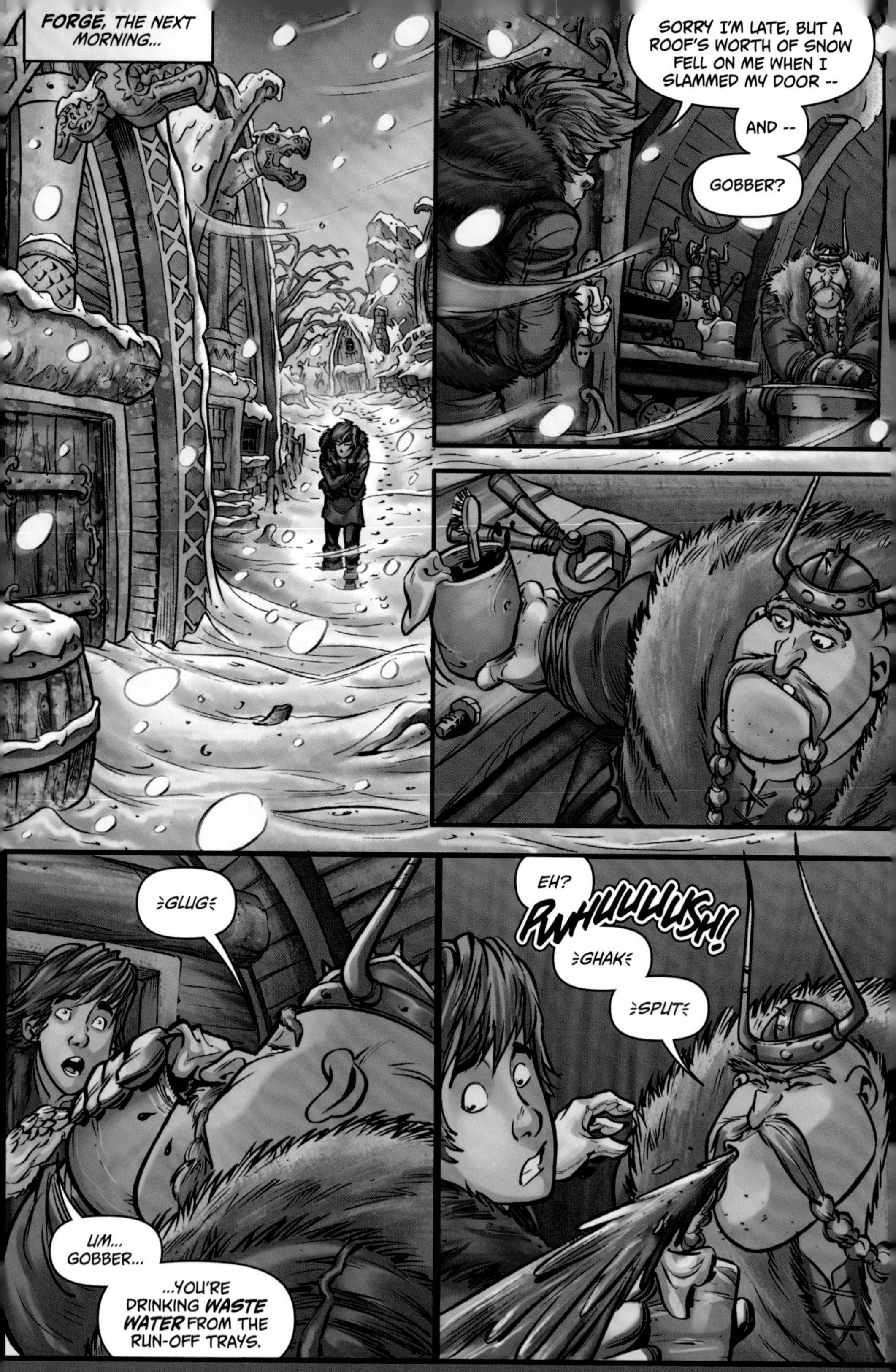
FORGE, THE NEXT MORNING...
SORRY I'M LATE, BUT A ROOF'S WORTH OF SNOW FELL ON ME WHEN I SLAMMED MY DOOR --
AND --
GOBBER?
GLUG
UM... GOBBER...
...YOU'RE DRINKING WASTE WATER FROM THE RUN-OFF TRAYS.
EH?
PWHUUUUSH!
GHAK
SPUT

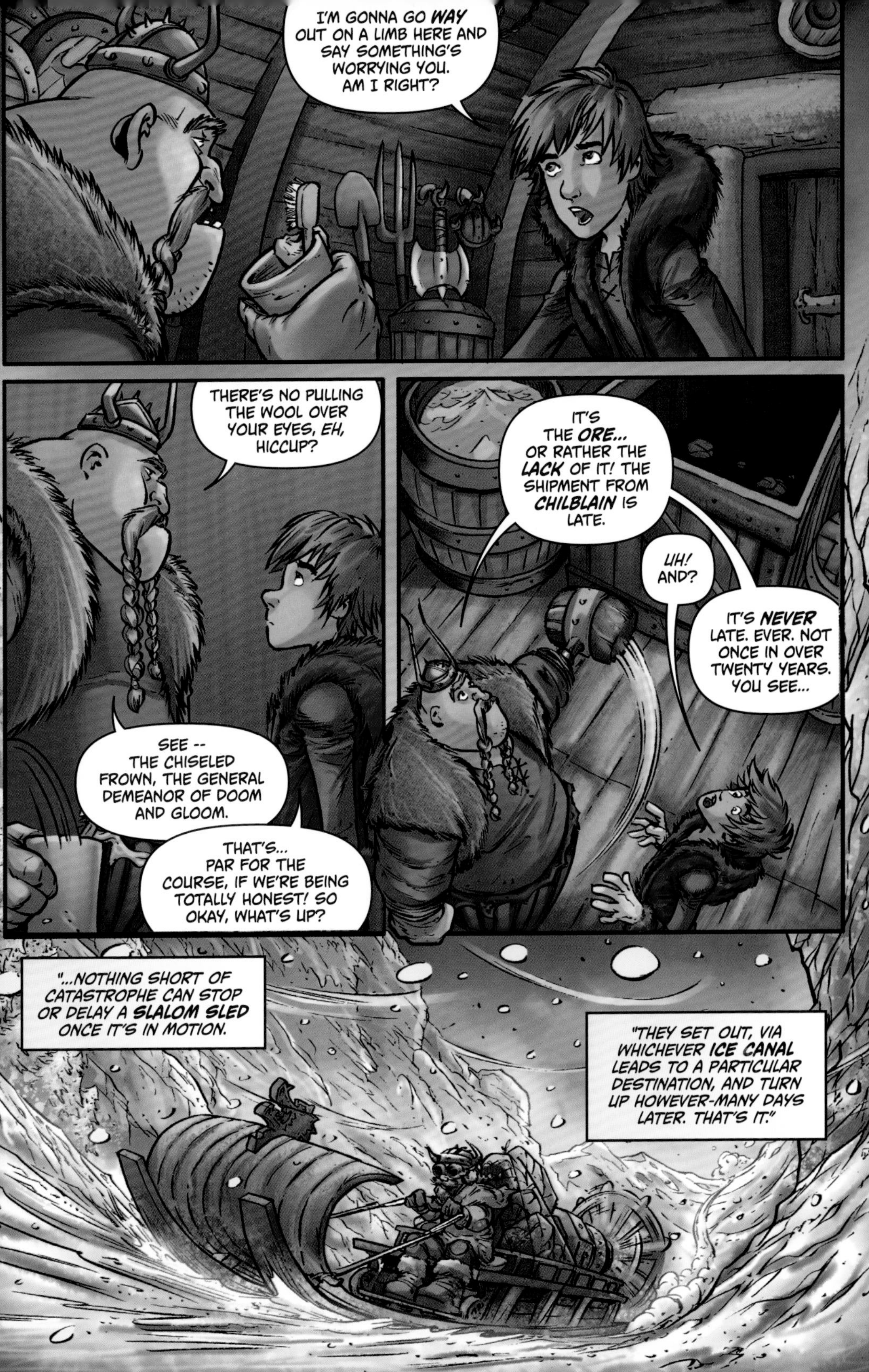

I'M GONNA GO WAY OUT ON A LIMB HERE AND SAY SOMETHING'S WORRYING YOU. AM I RIGHT?
THERE'S NO PULLING THE WOOL OVER YOUR EYES, EH, HICCUP?
SEE -- THE CHISELED FROWN, THE GENERAL DEMEANOR OF DOOM AND GLOOM.
THAT'S... PAR FOR THE COURSE, IF WE'RE BEING TOTALLY HONEST! SO OKAY, WHAT'S UP?
IT'S THE ORE... OR RATHER THE LACK OF IT! THE SHIPMENT FROM CHILBLAIN IS LATE.
UH! AND?
IT'S NEVER LATE. EVER. NOT ONCE IN OVER TWENTY YEARS. YOU SEE...
"...NOTHING SHORT OF CATASTROPHE CAN STOP OR DELAY A SLALOM SLED ONCE IT'S IN MOTION.
"THEY SET OUT, VIA WHICHEVER ICE CANAL LEADS TO A PARTICULAR DESTINATION, AND TURN UP HOWEVER-MANY DAYS LATER. THAT'S IT."

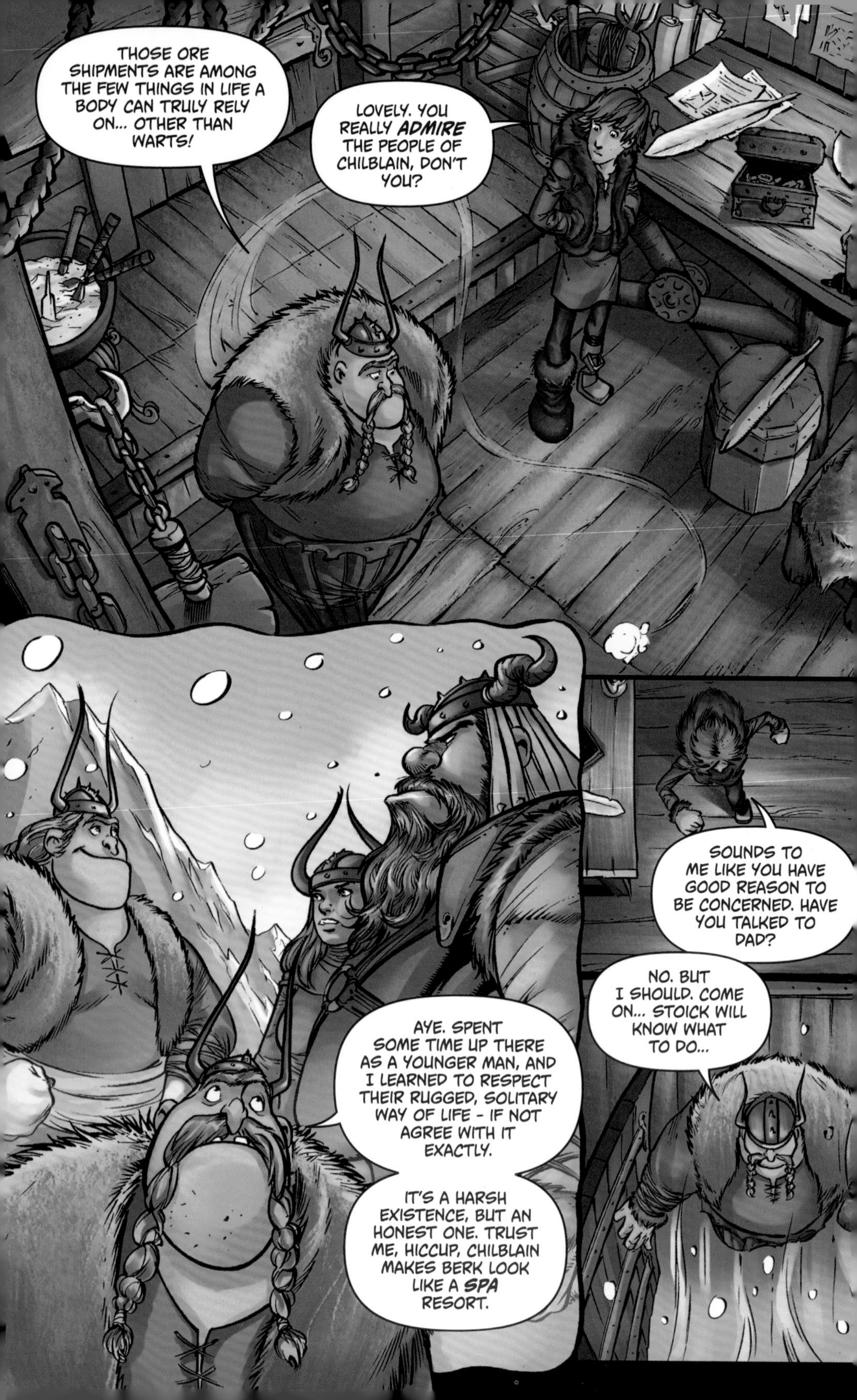
THOSE ORE SHIPMENTS ARE AMONG THE FEW THINGS IN LIFE A BODY CAN TRULY RELY ON... OTHER THAN WARTS!
LOVELY. YOU REALLY ADMIRE THE PEOPLE OF CHILBLAIN, DON'T YOU?
AYE. SPENT SOME TIME UP THERE AS A YOUNGER MAN, AND I LEARNED TO RESPECT THEIR RUGGED, SOLITARY WAY OF LIFE - IF NOT AGREE WITH IT EXACTLY.
IT'S A HARSH EXISTENCE, BUT AN HONEST ONE. TRUST ME, HICCUP, CHILBLAIN MAKES BERK LOOK LIKE A SPA RESORT.
SOUNDS TO ME LIKE YOU HAVE GOOD REASON TO BE CONCERNED. HAVE YOU TALKED TO DAD?
NO. BUT I SHOULD. COME ON... STOICK WILL KNOW WHAT TO DO...

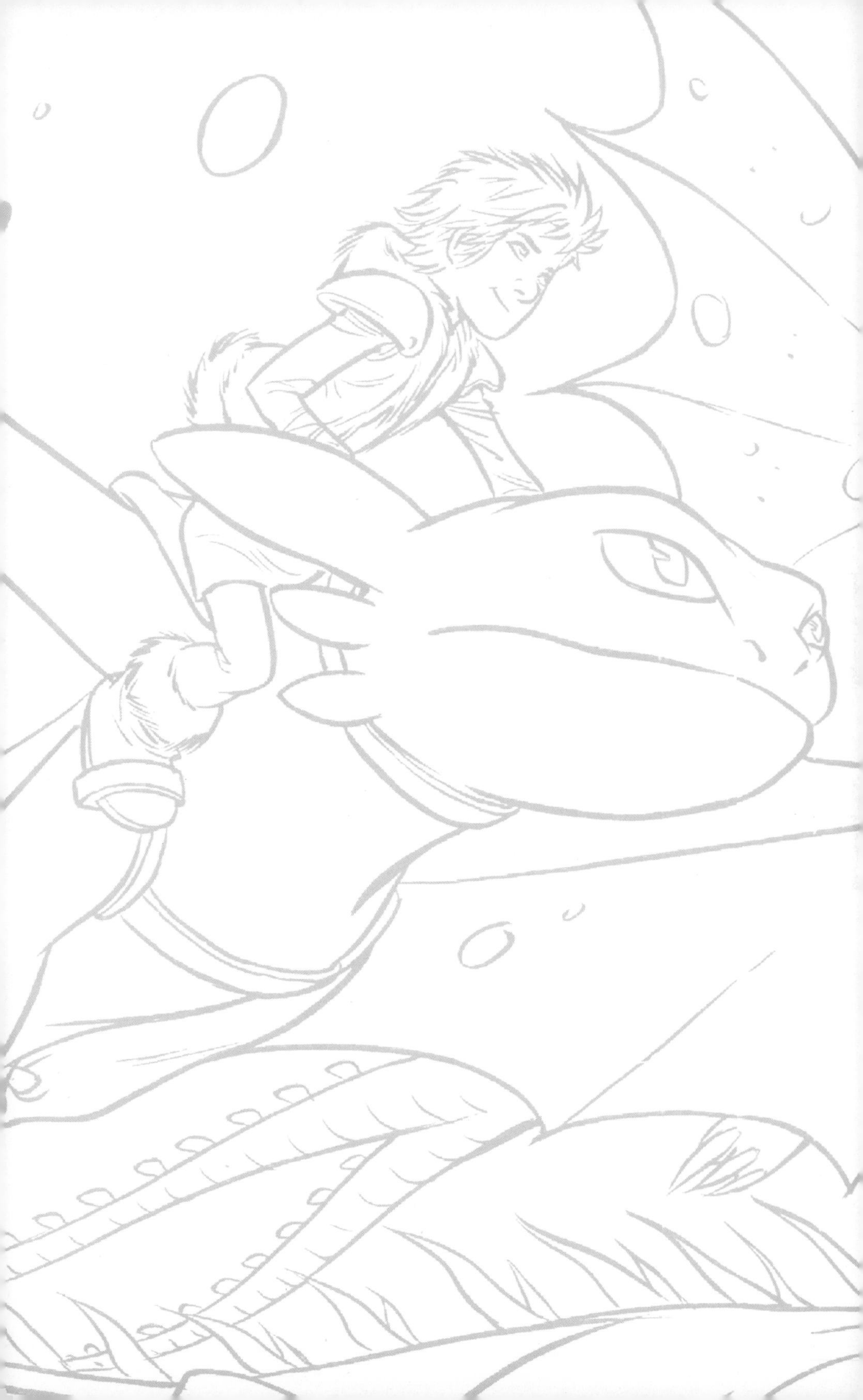

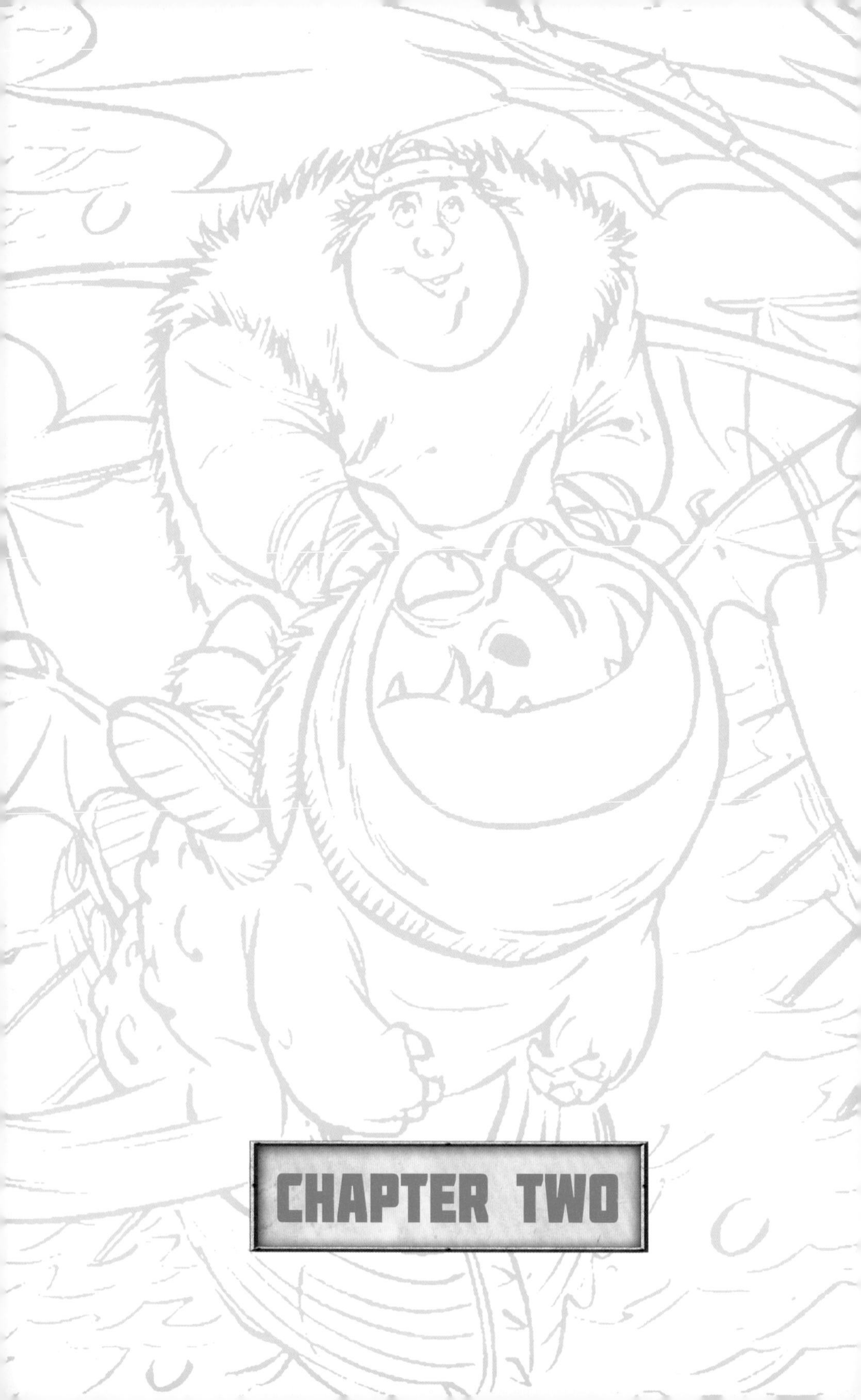

CHAPTER TWO

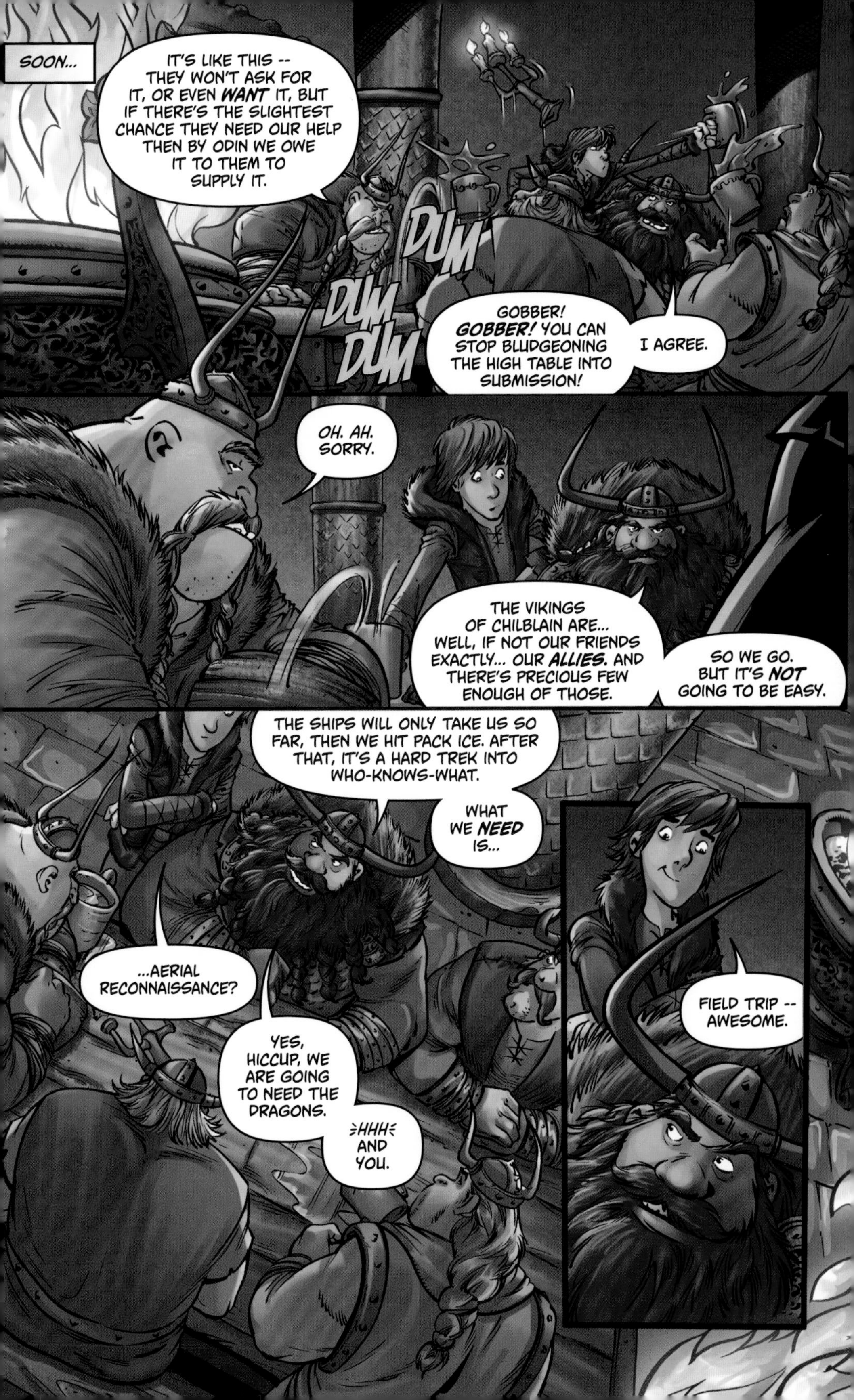
SOON...
IT'S LIKE THIS -- THEY WON'T ASK FOR IT, OR EVEN WANT IT, BUT IF THERE'S THE SLIGHTEST CHANCE THEY NEED OUR HELP THEN BY ODIN WE OWE IT TO THEM TO SUPPLY IT.
DUM DUM DUM
GOBBER! GOBBER! YOU CAN STOP BLUDGEONING THE HIGH TABLE INTO SUBMISSION!
I AGREE.
OH. AH. SORRY.
THE VIKINGS OF CHILBLAIN ARE... WELL, IF NOT OUR FRIENDS EXACTLY... OUR ALLIES. AND THERE'S PRECIOUS FEW ENOUGH OF THOSE.
SO WE GO. BUT IT'S NOT GOING TO BE EASY.
THE SHIPS WILL ONLY TAKE US SO FAR, THEN WE HIT PACK ICE. AFTER THAT, IT'S A HARD TREK INTO WHO-KNOWS-WHAT.
WHAT WE NEED IS...
...AERIAL RECONNAISSANCE?
YES, HICCUP, WE ARE GOING TO NEED THE DRAGONS.
HHH AND YOU.
FIELD TRIP -- AWESOME.

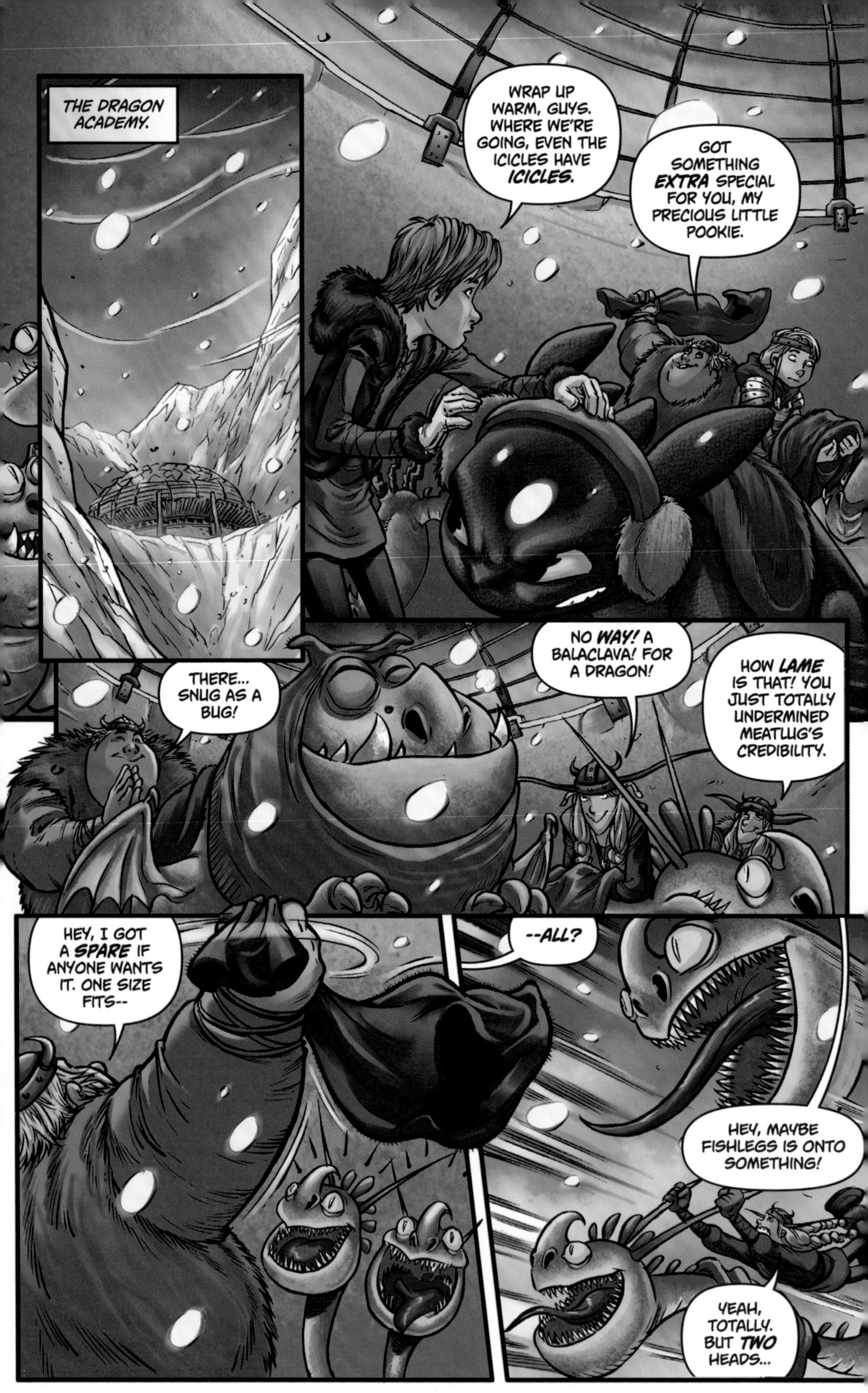
THE DRAGON ACADEMY.
WRAP UP WARM, GUYS. WHERE WE'RE GOING, EVEN THE ICICLES HAVE ICICLES.
GOT SOMETHING EXTRA SPECIAL FOR YOU, MY PRECIOUS LITTLE POOKIE.
THERE... SNUG AS A BUG!
NO WAY! A BALACLAVA! FOR A DRAGON!
HOW LAME IS THAT! YOU JUST TOTALLY UNDERMINED MEATLUG'S CREDIBILITY.
HEY, I GOT A SPARE IF ANYONE WANTS IT. ONE SIZE FITS--
--ALL?
HEY, MAYBE FISHLEGS IS ONTO SOMETHING!
YEAH, TOTALLY. BUT TWO HEADS...

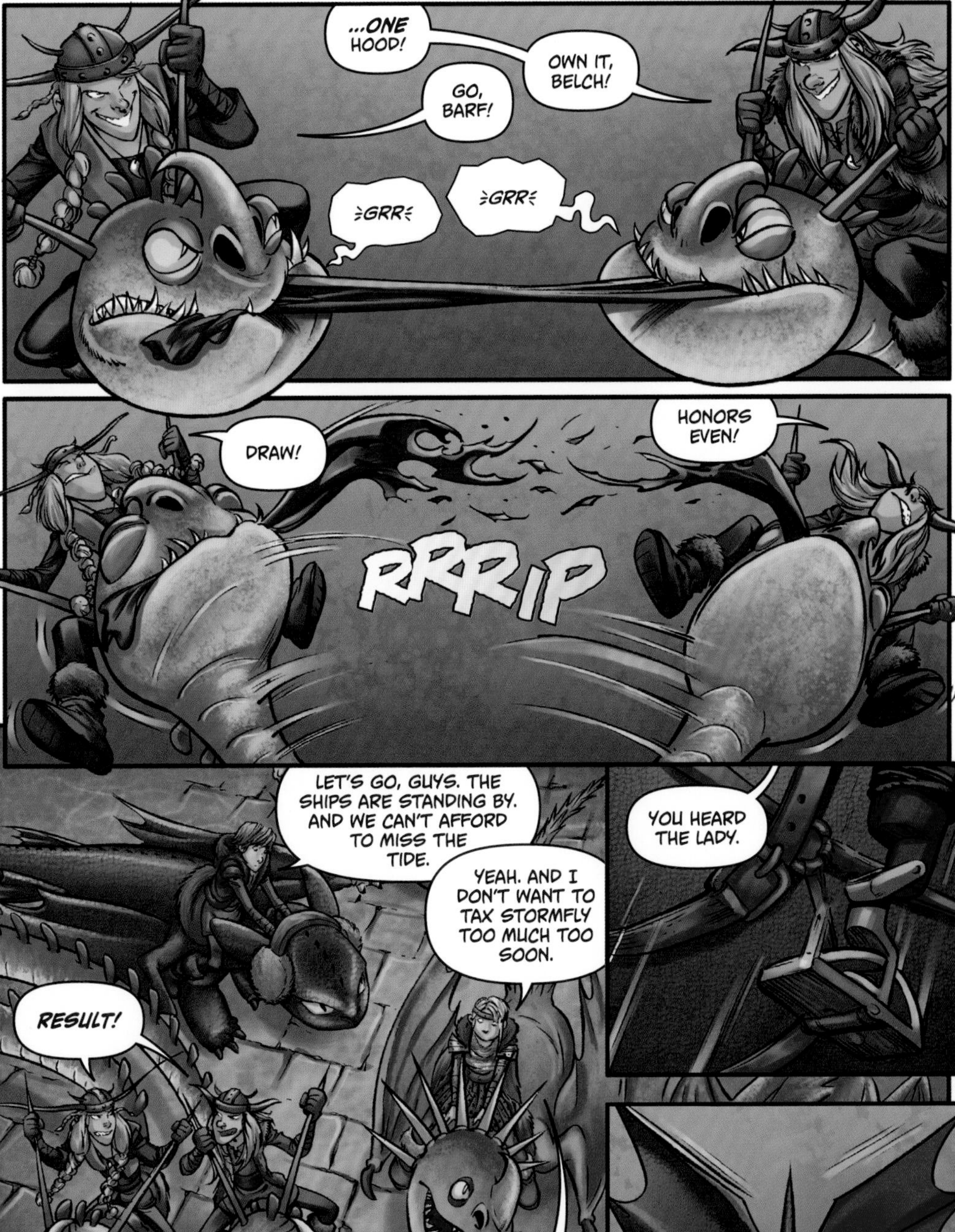
...ONE HOOD!
OWN IT, BELCH!
GO, BARF!
GRR
GRR
DRAW!
HONORS EVEN!
RRRIP
LET'S GO, GUYS. THE SHIPS ARE STANDING BY. AND WE CAN'T AFFORD TO MISS THE TIDE.
YEAH. AND I DON'T WANT TO TAX STORMFLY TOO MUCH TOO SOON.
RESULT!
SO HUSTLE.
SSPUT
YOU HEARD THE LADY.
TOOTHLESS --

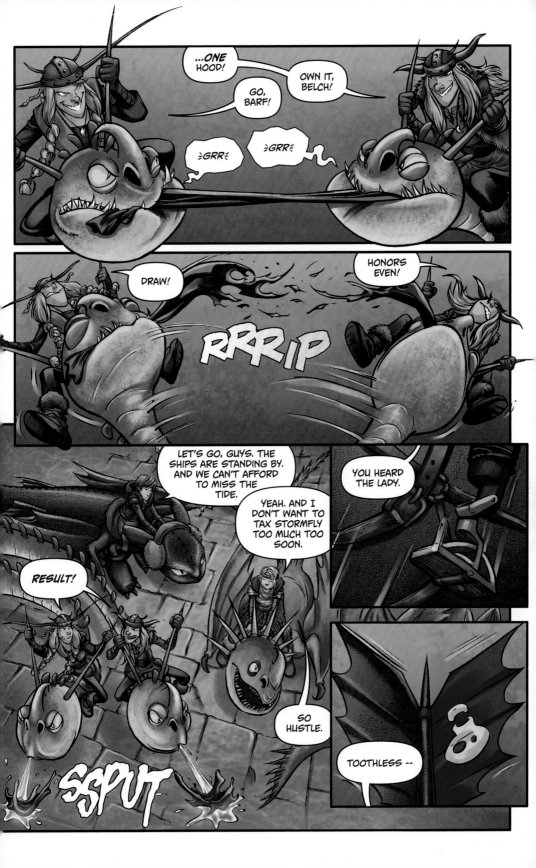

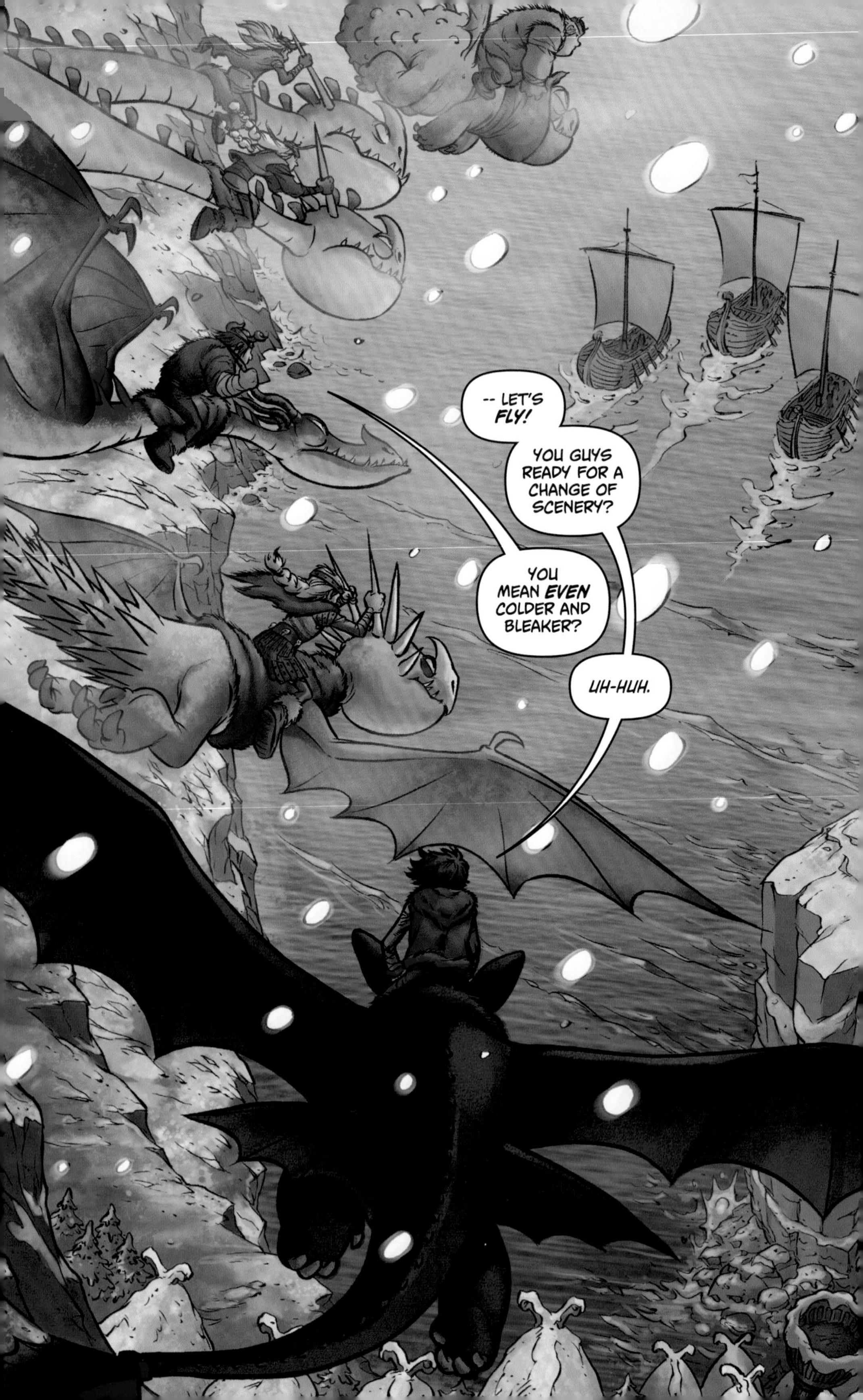
-- LET'S FLY!
YOU GUYS READY FOR A CHANGE OF SCENERY?
YOU MEAN EVEN COLDER AND BLEAKER?
UH-HUH.

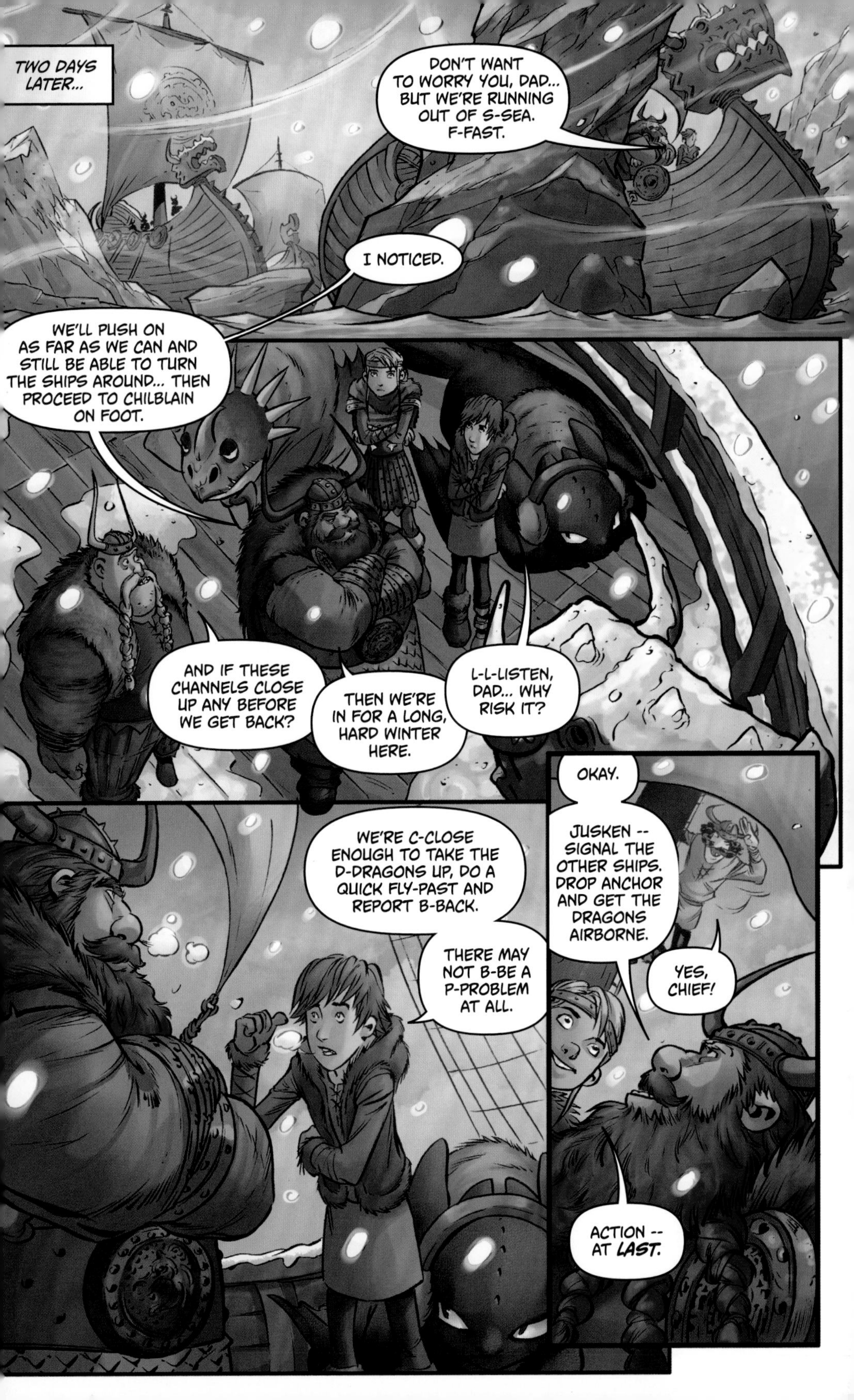
TWO DAYS LATER...
DON'T WANT TO WORRY YOU, DAD... BUT WE'RE RUNNING OUT OF S-SEA. F-FAST.
I NOTICED.
WE'LL PUSH ON AS FAR AS WE CAN AND STILL BE ABLE TO TURN THE SHIPS AROUND... THEN PROCEED TO CHILBLAIN ON FOOT.
AND IF THESE CHANNELS CLOSE UP ANY BEFORE WE GET BACK?
THEN WE'RE IN FOR A LONG, HARD WINTER HERE.
L-L-LISTEN, DAD... WHY RISK IT?
WE'RE C-CLOSE ENOUGH TO TAKE THE D-DRAGONS UP, DO A QUICK FLY-PAST AND REPORT B-BACK.
THERE MAY NOT B-BE A P-PROBLEM AT ALL.
OKAY.
JUSKEN -- SIGNAL THE OTHER SHIPS. DROP ANCHOR AND GET THE DRAGONS AIRBORNE.
YES, CHIEF!
ACTION -- AT **LAST**.

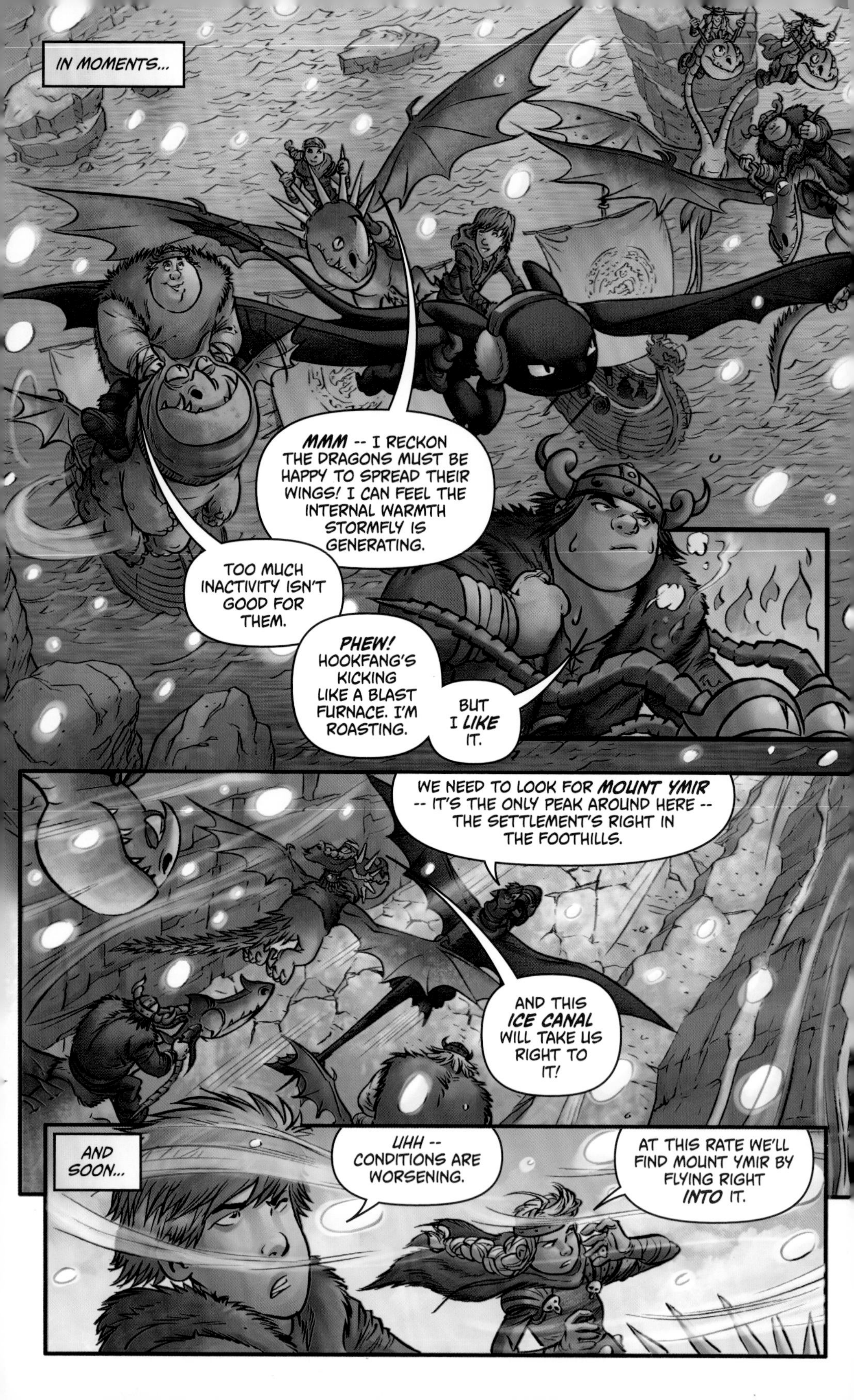
IN MOMENTS...
MMM -- I RECKON THE DRAGONS MUST BE HAPPY TO SPREAD THEIR WINGS! I CAN FEEL THE INTERNAL WARMTH STORMFLY IS GENERATING.
TOO MUCH INACTIVITY ISN'T GOOD FOR THEM.
PHEW! HOOKFANG'S KICKING LIKE A BLAST FURNACE. I'M ROASTING.
BUT I LIKE IT.
WE NEED TO LOOK FOR MOUNT YMIR -- IT'S THE ONLY PEAK AROUND HERE -- THE SETTLEMENT'S RIGHT IN THE FOOTHILLS.
AND THIS ICE CANAL WILL TAKE US RIGHT TO IT!
AND SOON...
UHH -- CONDITIONS ARE WORSENING.
AT THIS RATE WE'LL FIND MOUNT YMIR BY FLYING RIGHT INTO IT.

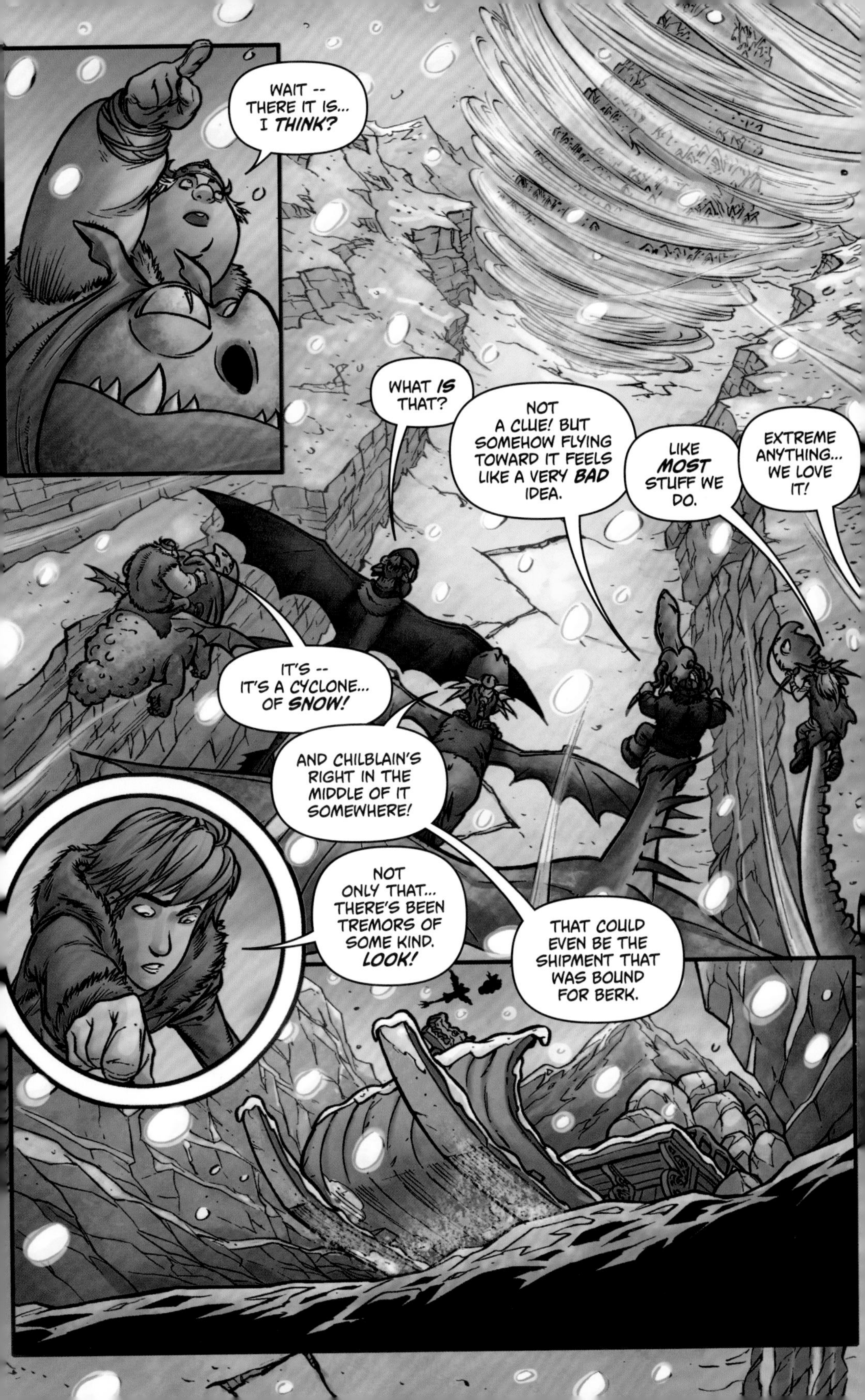

WAIT -- THERE IT IS... I *THINK?*
WHAT *IS* THAT?
NOT A CLUE! BUT SOMEHOW FLYING TOWARD IT FEELS LIKE A VERY *BAD* IDEA.
LIKE *MOST* STUFF WE DO.
EXTREME ANYTHING... WE LOVE IT!
IT'S -- IT'S A CYCLONE... OF *SNOW!*
AND CHILBLAIN'S RIGHT IN THE MIDDLE OF IT SOMEWHERE!
NOT ONLY THAT... THERE'S BEEN TREMORS OF SOME KIND. *LOOK!*
THAT COULD EVEN BE THE SHIPMENT THAT WAS BOUND FOR BERK.

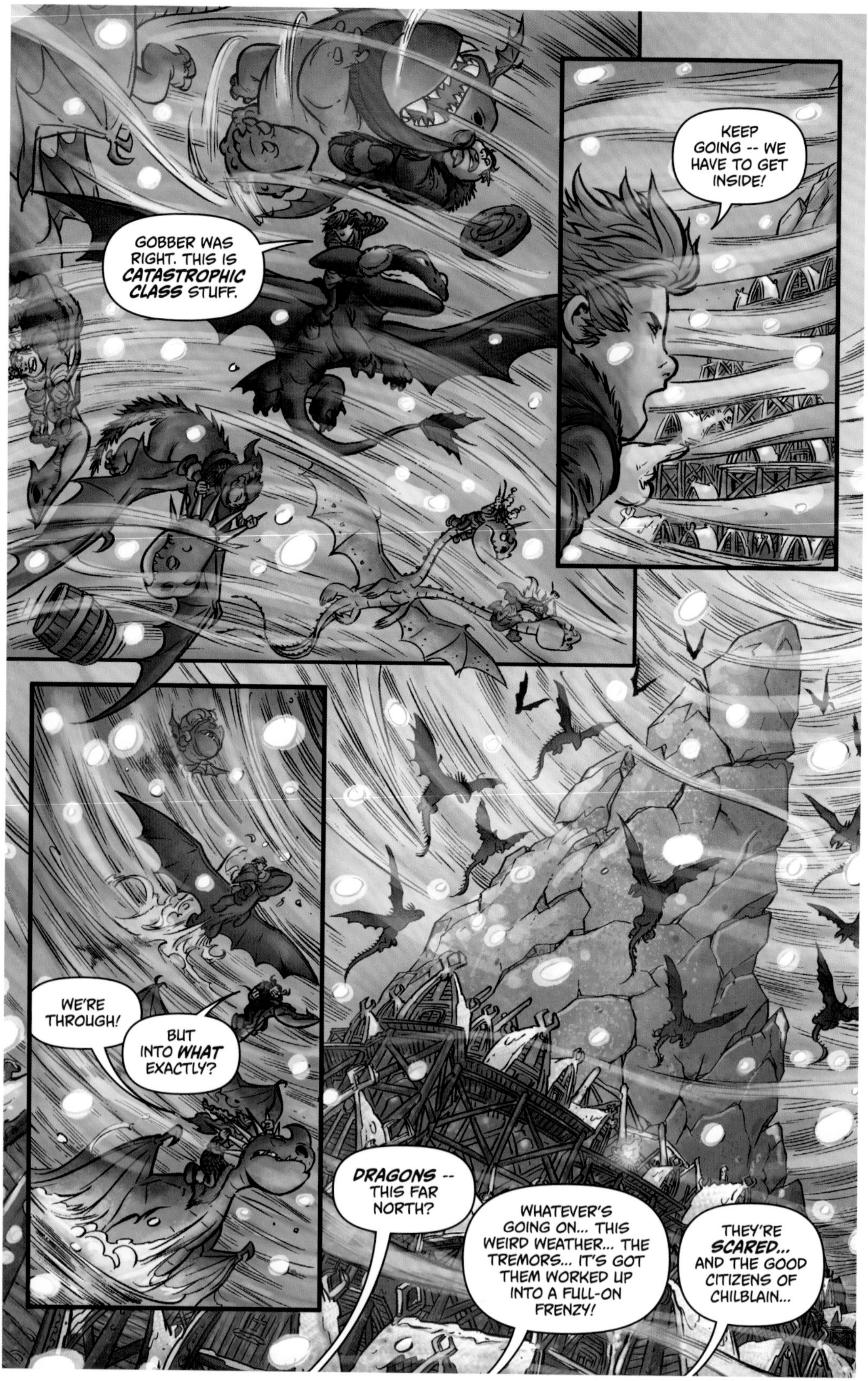
GOBBER WAS RIGHT. THIS IS CATASTROPHIC CLASS STUFF.
KEEP GOING -- WE HAVE TO GET INSIDE!
WE'RE THROUGH!
BUT INTO WHAT EXACTLY?
DRAGONS -- THIS FAR NORTH?
WHATEVER'S GOING ON... THIS WEIRD WEATHER... THE TREMORS... IT'S GOT THEM WORKED UP INTO A FULL-ON FRENZY!
THEY'RE SCARED... AND THE GOOD CITIZENS OF CHILBLAIN...

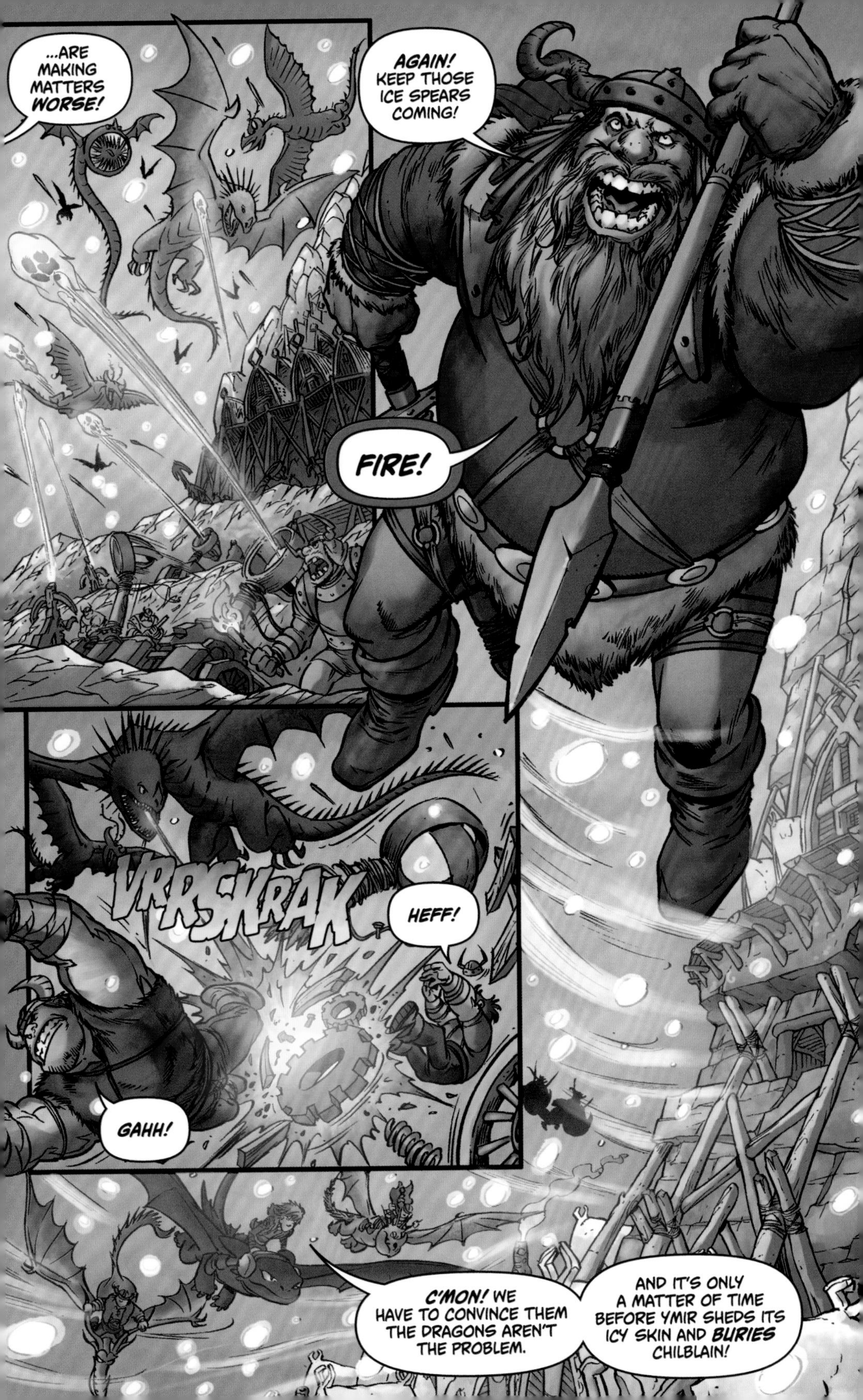
...ARE MAKING MATTERS WORSE!
AGAIN! KEEP THOSE ICE SPEARS COMING!
FIRE!
VRRSKRAK
HEFF!
GAHH!
C'MON! WE HAVE TO CONVINCE THEM THE DRAGONS AREN'T THE PROBLEM.
AND IT'S ONLY A MATTER OF TIME BEFORE YMIR SHEDS ITS ICY SKIN AND BURIES CHILBLAIN!

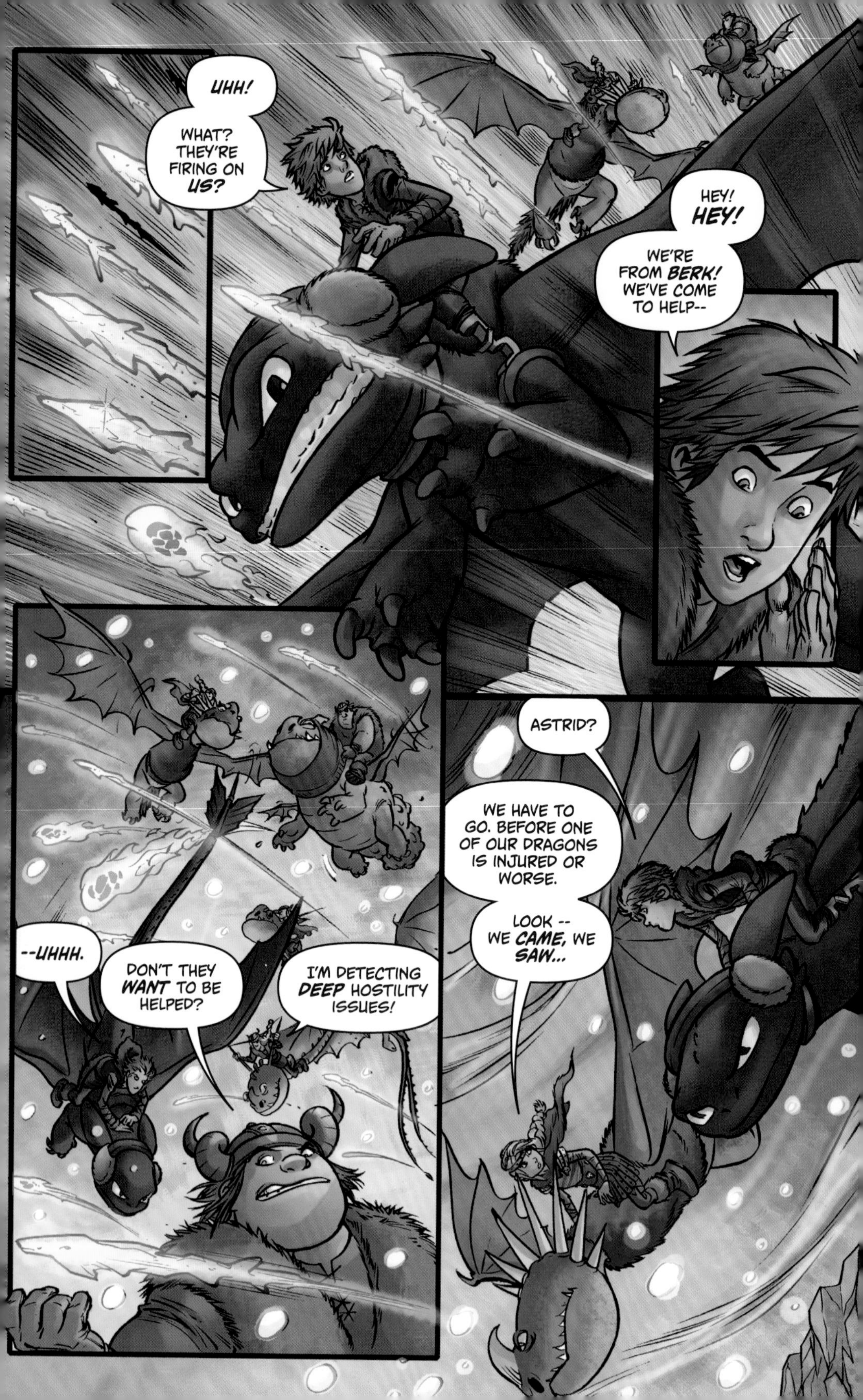
UHH!
WHAT? THEY'RE FIRING ON US?
HEY! HEY!
WE'RE FROM BERK! WE'VE COME TO HELP--
--UHHH.
DON'T THEY WANT TO BE HELPED?
I'M DETECTING DEEP HOSTILITY ISSUES!
ASTRID?
WE HAVE TO GO. BEFORE ONE OF OUR DRAGONS IS INJURED OR WORSE.
LOOK -- WE CAME, WE SAW...

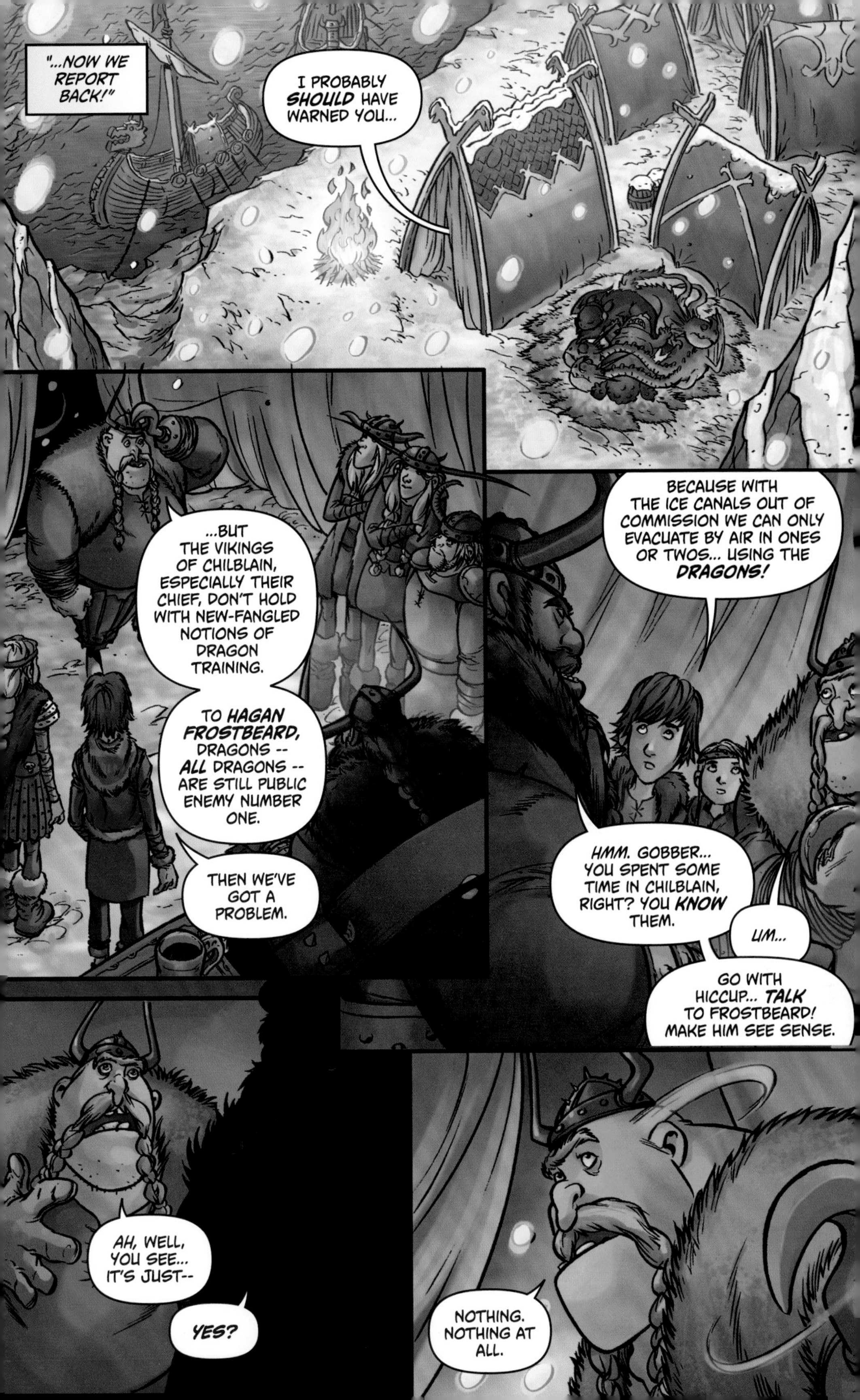
"...NOW WE REPORT BACK!"
I PROBABLY SHOULD HAVE WARNED YOU...
...BUT THE VIKINGS OF CHILBLAIN, ESPECIALLY THEIR CHIEF, DON'T HOLD WITH NEW-FANGLED NOTIONS OF DRAGON TRAINING.
TO HAGAN FROSTBEARD, DRAGONS -- ALL DRAGONS -- ARE STILL PUBLIC ENEMY NUMBER ONE.
THEN WE'VE GOT A PROBLEM.
BECAUSE WITH THE ICE CANALS OUT OF COMMISSION WE CAN ONLY EVACUATE BY AIR IN ONES OR TWOS... USING THE DRAGONS!
HMM. GOBBER... YOU SPENT SOME TIME IN CHILBLAIN, RIGHT? YOU KNOW THEM.
UM...
GO WITH HICCUP... TALK TO FROSTBEARD! MAKE HIM SEE SENSE.
AH, WELL, YOU SEE... IT'S JUST--
YES?
NOTHING. NOTHING AT ALL.

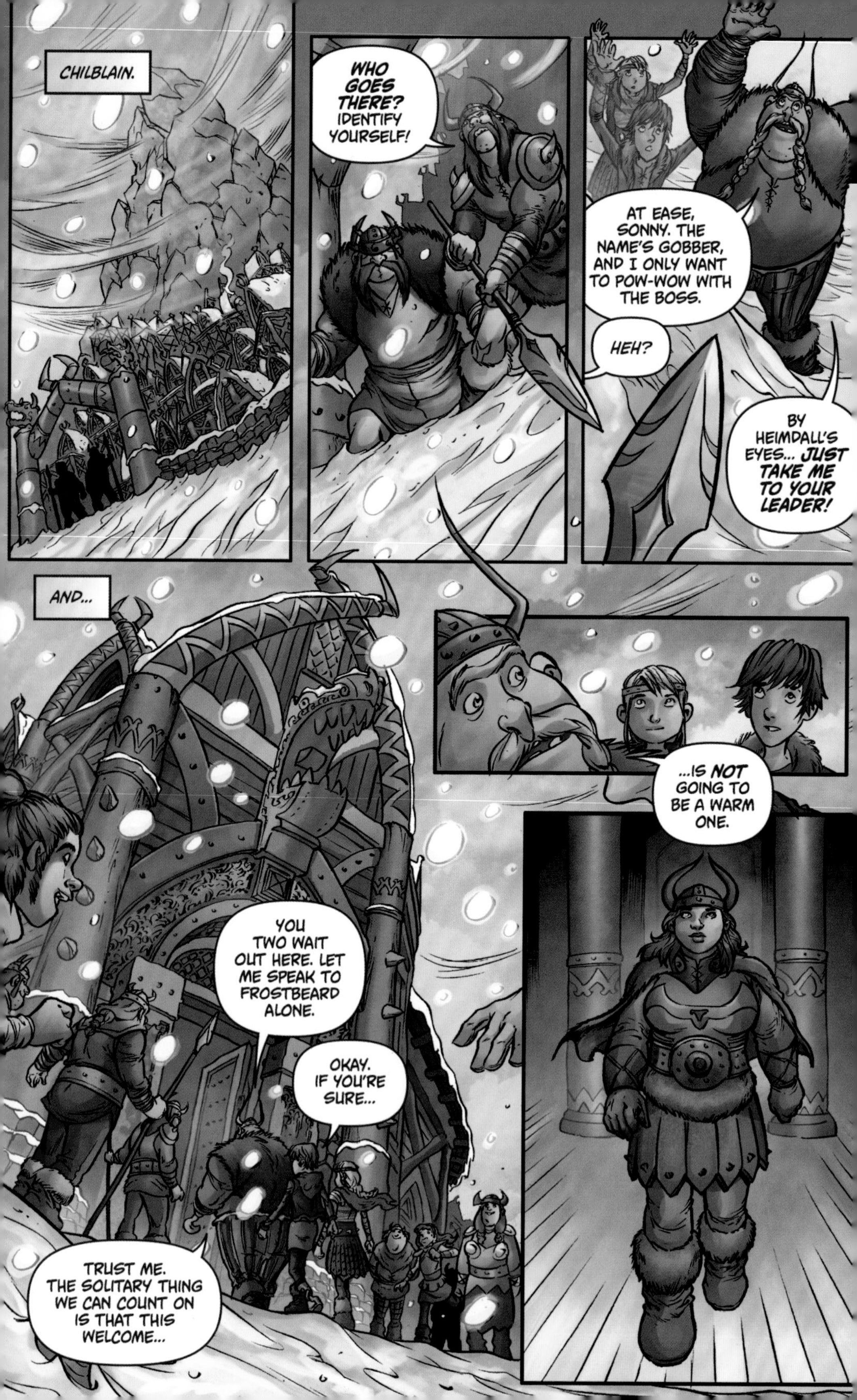
CHILBLAIN.
WHO GOES THERE? IDENTIFY YOURSELF!
AT EASE, SONNY. THE NAME'S GOBBER, AND I ONLY WANT TO POW-WOW WITH THE BOSS.
HEH?
BY HEIMDALL'S EYES... JUST TAKE ME TO YOUR LEADER!
AND...
YOU TWO WAIT OUT HERE. LET ME SPEAK TO FROSTBEARD ALONE.
OKAY. IF YOU'RE SURE...
TRUST ME. THE SOLITARY THING WE CAN COUNT ON IS THAT THIS WELCOME...
...IS NOT GOING TO BE A WARM ONE.

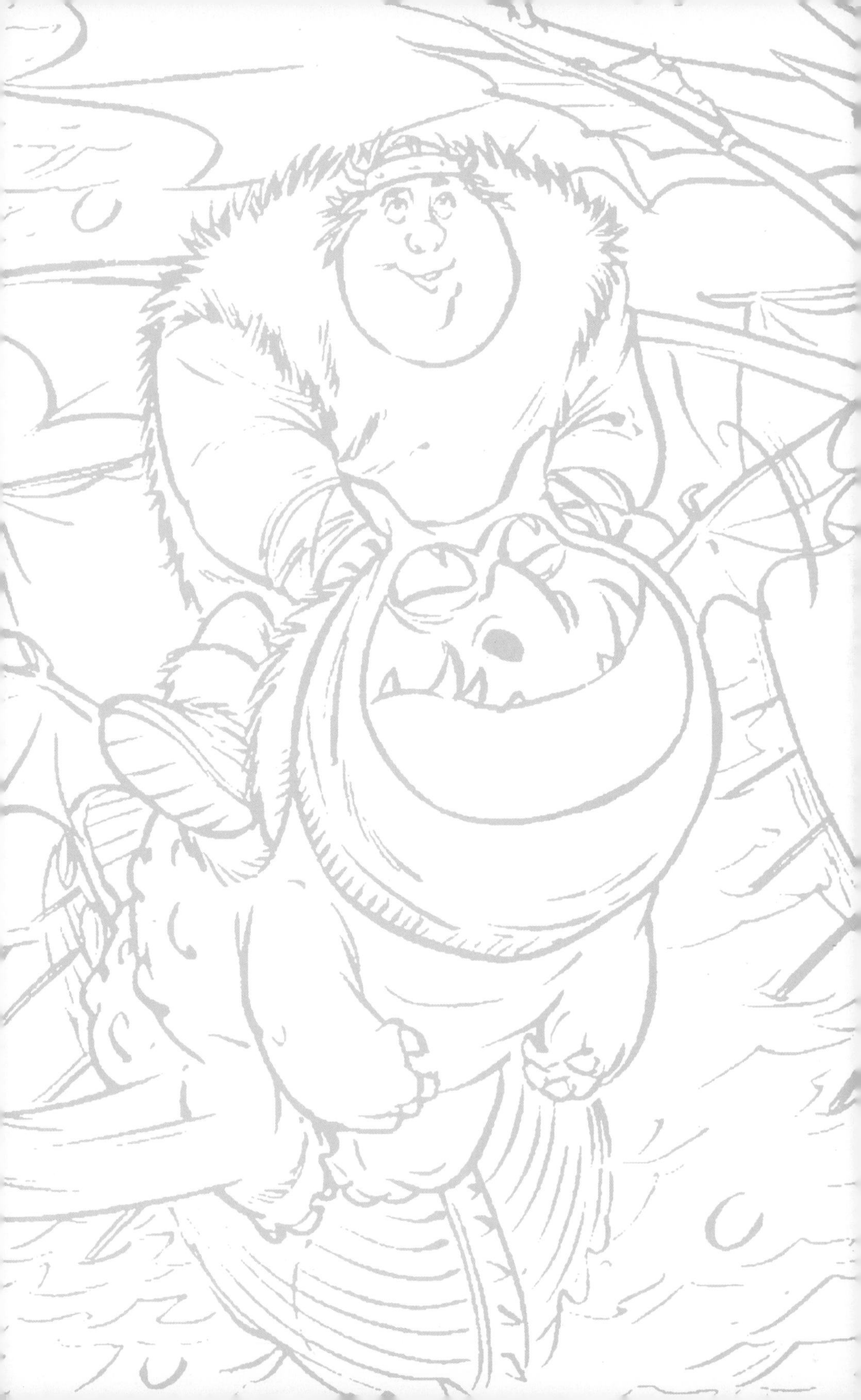

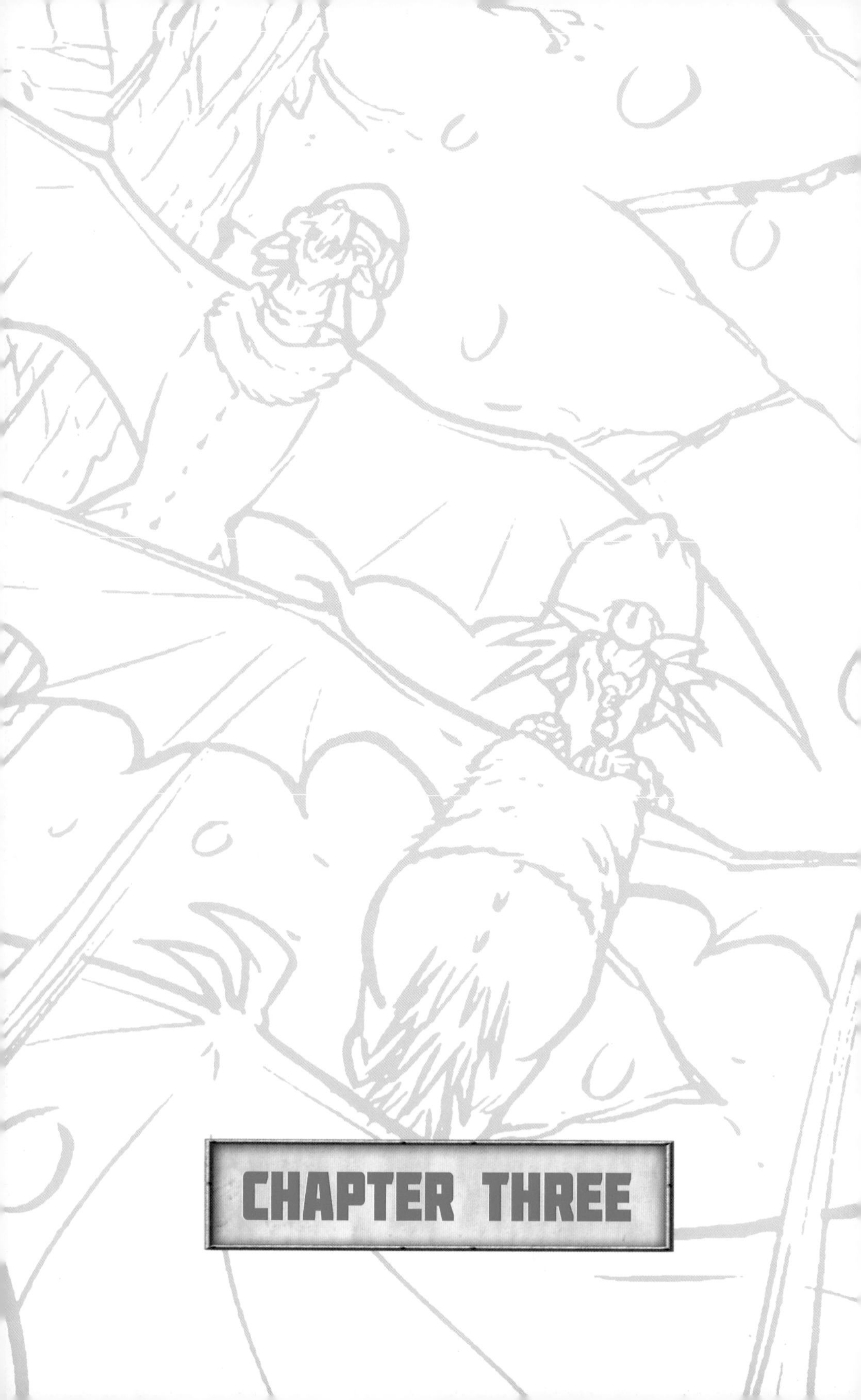

CHAPTER THREE

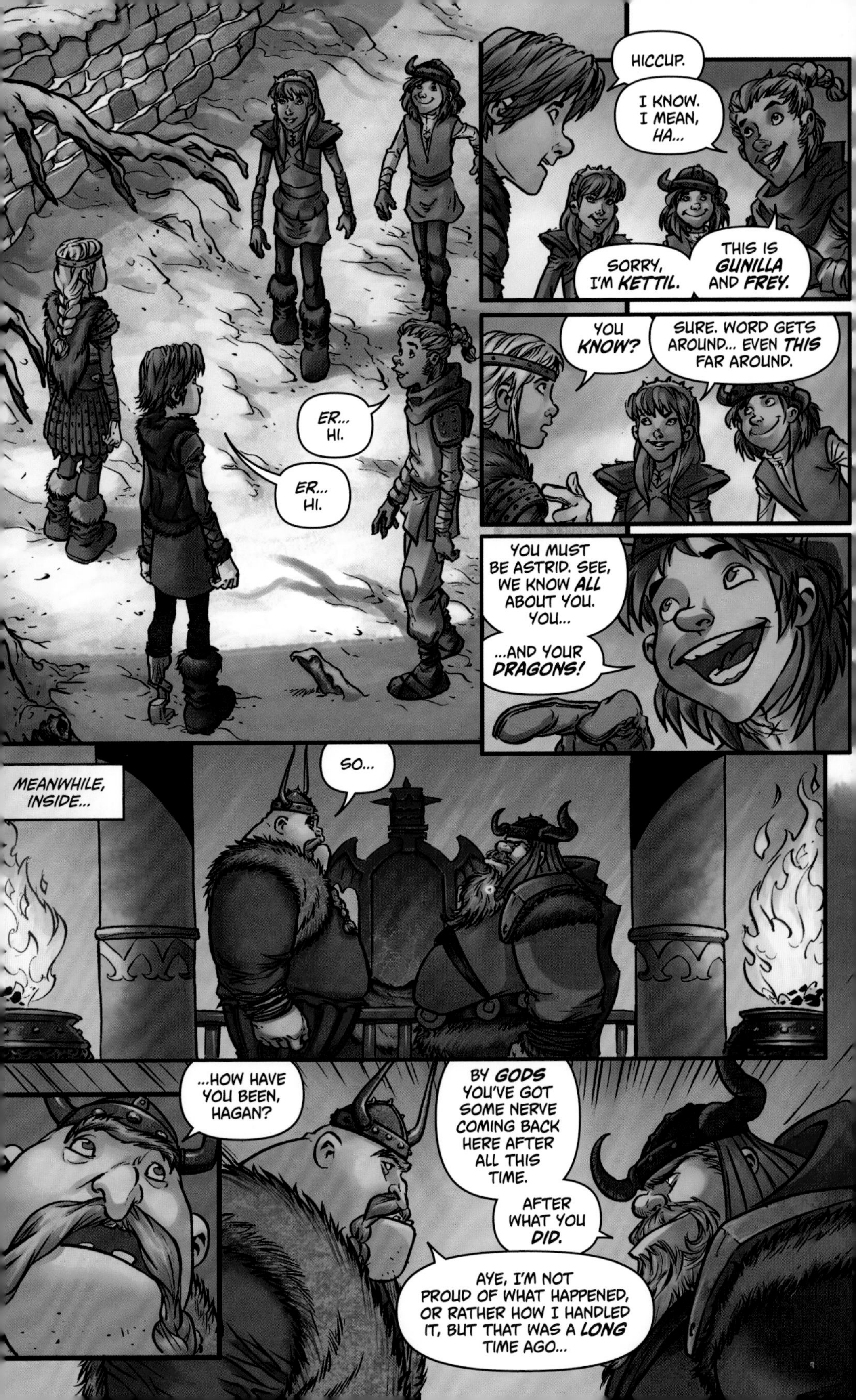
ER... HI.
ER... HI.
HICCUP.
I KNOW. I MEAN, HA...
SORRY, I'M KETTIL.
THIS IS GUNILLA AND FREY.
YOU KNOW?
SURE. WORD GETS AROUND... EVEN THIS FAR AROUND.
YOU MUST BE ASTRID. SEE, WE KNOW ALL ABOUT YOU. YOU...
...AND YOUR DRAGONS!
MEANWHILE, INSIDE...
SO...
...HOW HAVE YOU BEEN, HAGAN?
BY GODS YOU'VE GOT SOME NERVE COMING BACK HERE AFTER ALL THIS TIME.
AFTER WHAT YOU DID.
AYE, I'M NOT PROUD OF WHAT HAPPENED, OR RATHER HOW I HANDLED IT, BUT THAT WAS A LONG TIME AGO...

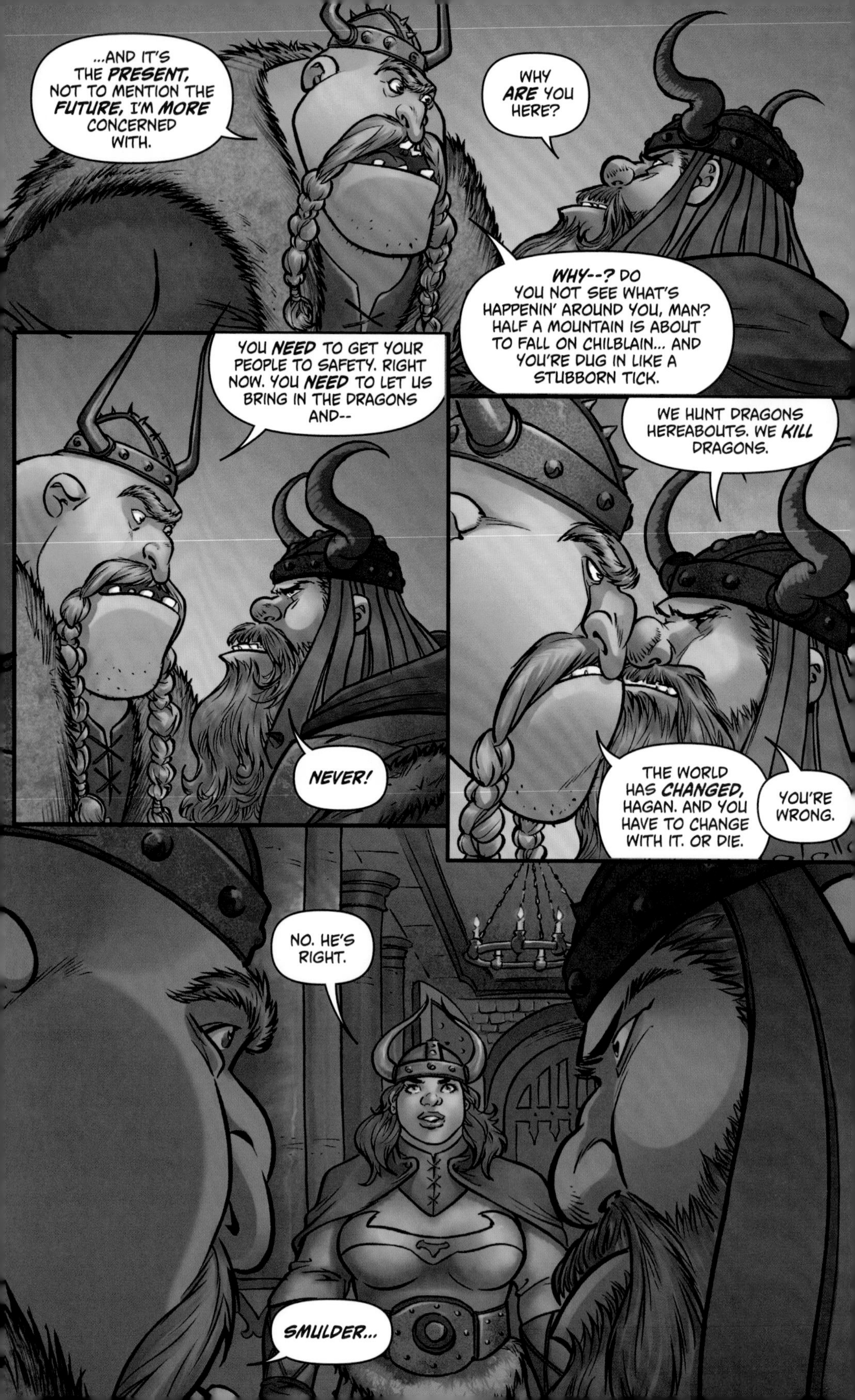
...AND IT'S THE PRESENT, NOT TO MENTION THE FUTURE, I'M MORE CONCERNED WITH.
WHY ARE YOU HERE?
WHY--? DO YOU NOT SEE WHAT'S HAPPENIN' AROUND YOU, MAN? HALF A MOUNTAIN IS ABOUT TO FALL ON CHILBLAIN... AND YOU'RE DUG IN LIKE A STUBBORN TICK.
YOU NEED TO GET YOUR PEOPLE TO SAFETY. RIGHT NOW. YOU NEED TO LET US BRING IN THE DRAGONS AND--
NEVER!
WE HUNT DRAGONS HEREABOUTS. WE KILL DRAGONS.
THE WORLD HAS CHANGED, HAGAN. AND YOU HAVE TO CHANGE WITH IT. OR DIE.
YOU'RE WRONG.
NO. HE'S RIGHT.
SMULDER...

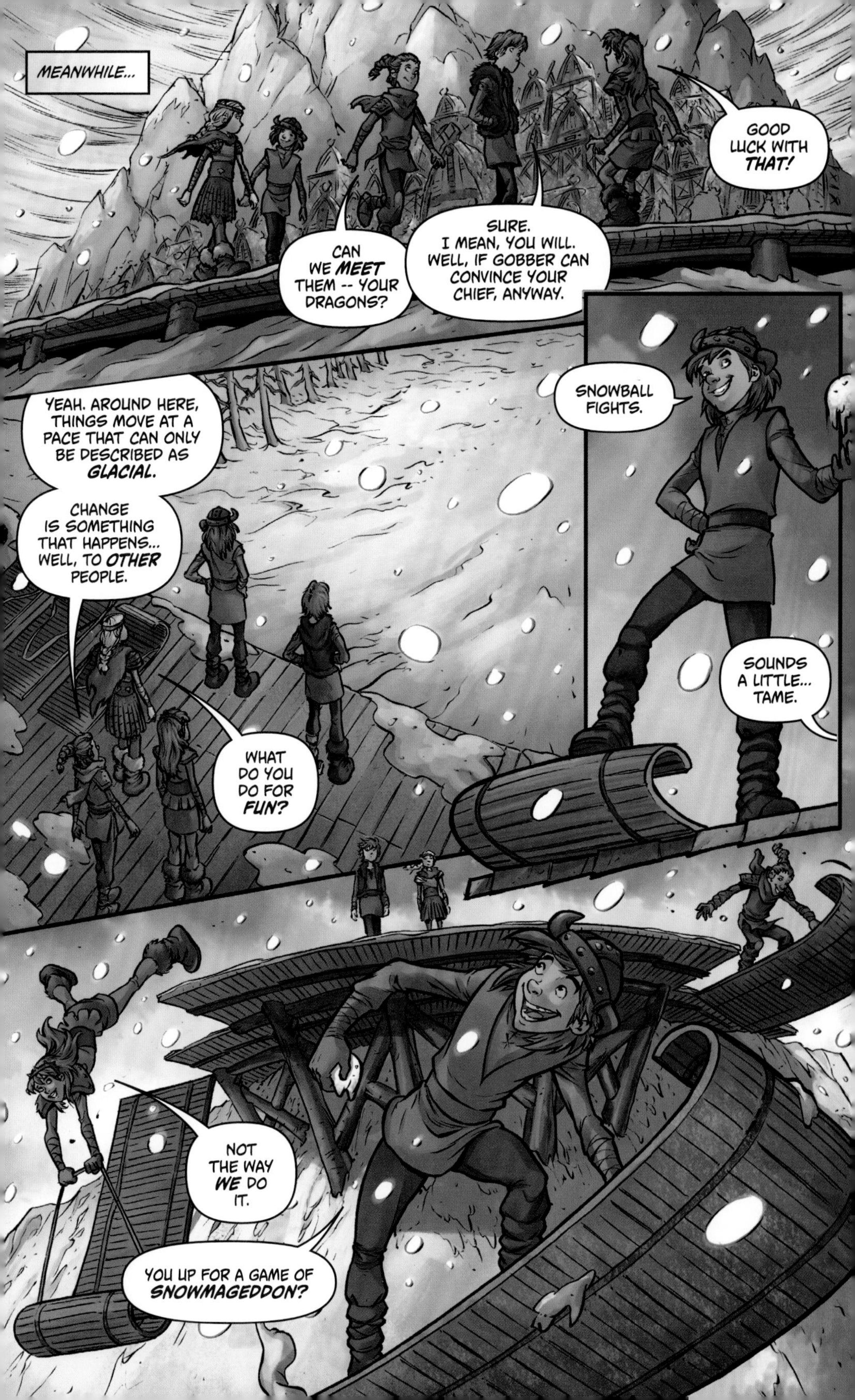
MEANWHILE...
GOOD LUCK WITH *THAT!*
CAN WE *MEET* THEM -- YOUR DRAGONS?
SURE. I MEAN, YOU WILL. WELL, IF GOBBER CAN CONVINCE YOUR CHIEF, ANYWAY.
YEAH. AROUND HERE, THINGS MOVE AT A PACE THAT CAN ONLY BE DESCRIBED AS *GLACIAL.*
CHANGE IS SOMETHING THAT HAPPENS... WELL, TO *OTHER* PEOPLE.
WHAT DO YOU DO FOR *FUN?*
SNOWBALL FIGHTS.
SOUNDS A LITTLE... TAME.
NOT THE WAY *WE* DO IT.
YOU UP FOR A GAME OF *SNOWMAGEDDON?*

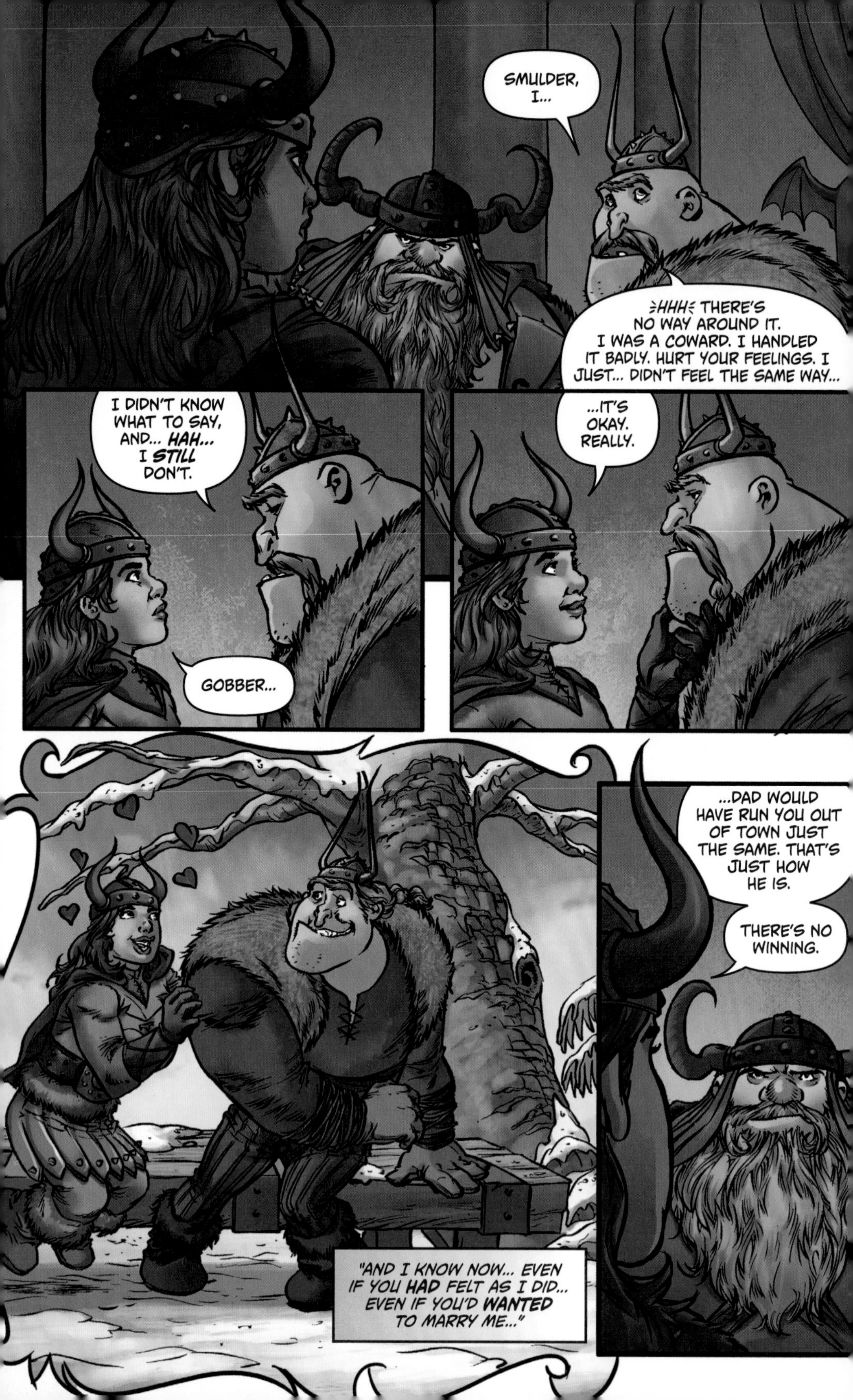
SMULDER, I...
HHH THERE'S NO WAY AROUND IT. I WAS A COWARD. I HANDLED IT BADLY. HURT YOUR FEELINGS. I JUST... DIDN'T FEEL THE SAME WAY...
I DIDN'T KNOW WHAT TO SAY, AND... HAH... I STILL DON'T.
GOBBER...
...IT'S OKAY. REALLY.
"AND I KNOW NOW... EVEN IF YOU HAD FELT AS I DID... EVEN IF YOU'D WANTED TO MARRY ME..."
...DAD WOULD HAVE RUN YOU OUT OF TOWN JUST THE SAME. THAT'S JUST HOW HE IS.
THERE'S NO WINNING.

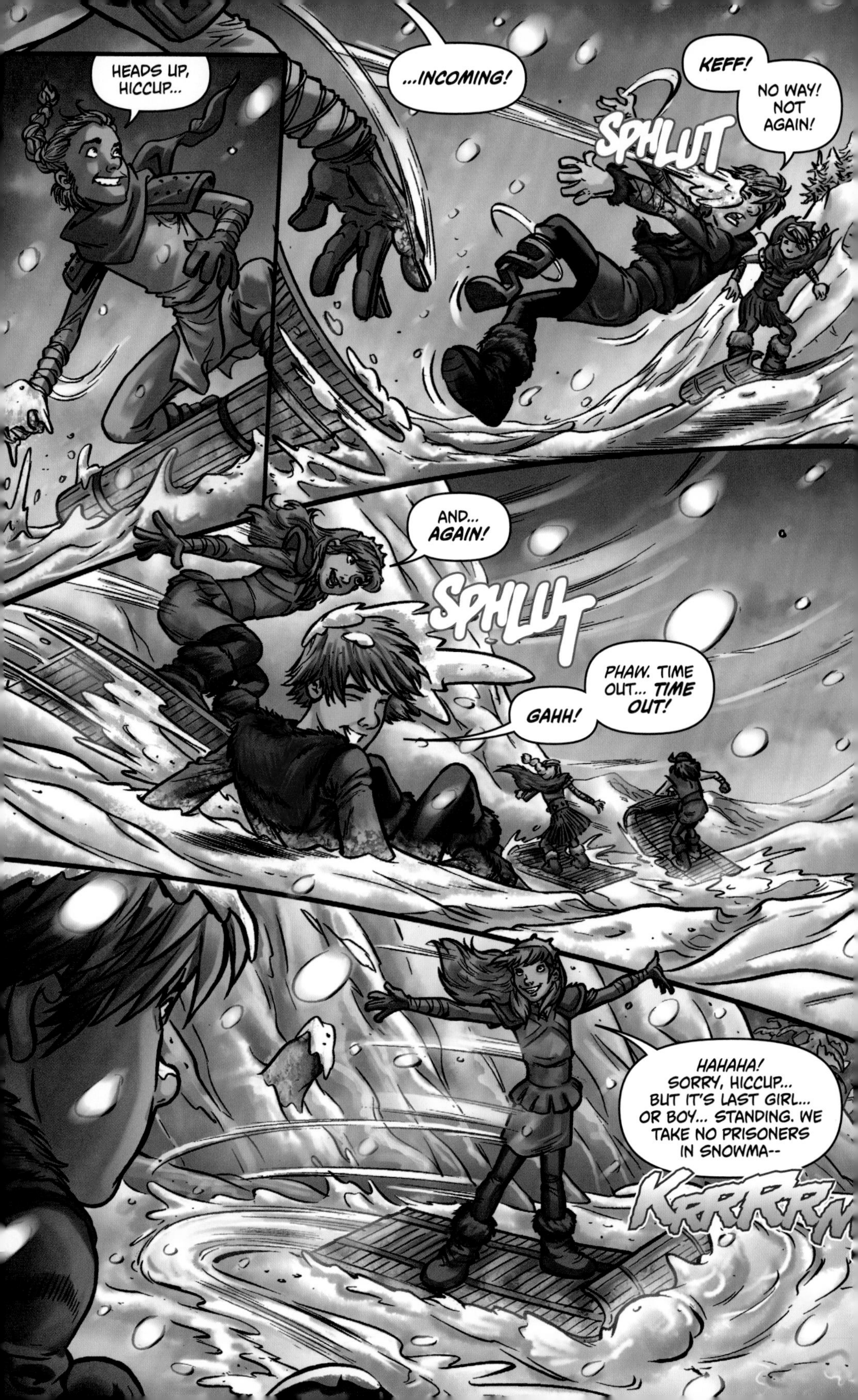
HEADS UP, HICCUP...
...INCOMING!
KEFF!
SPHLUT
NO WAY! NOT AGAIN!
AND... AGAIN!
SPHLUT
GAHH!
PHAW. TIME OUT... TIME OUT!
HAHAHA! SORRY, HICCUP... BUT IT'S LAST GIRL... OR BOY... STANDING. WE TAKE NO PRISONERS IN SNOWMA--
KRRRRM

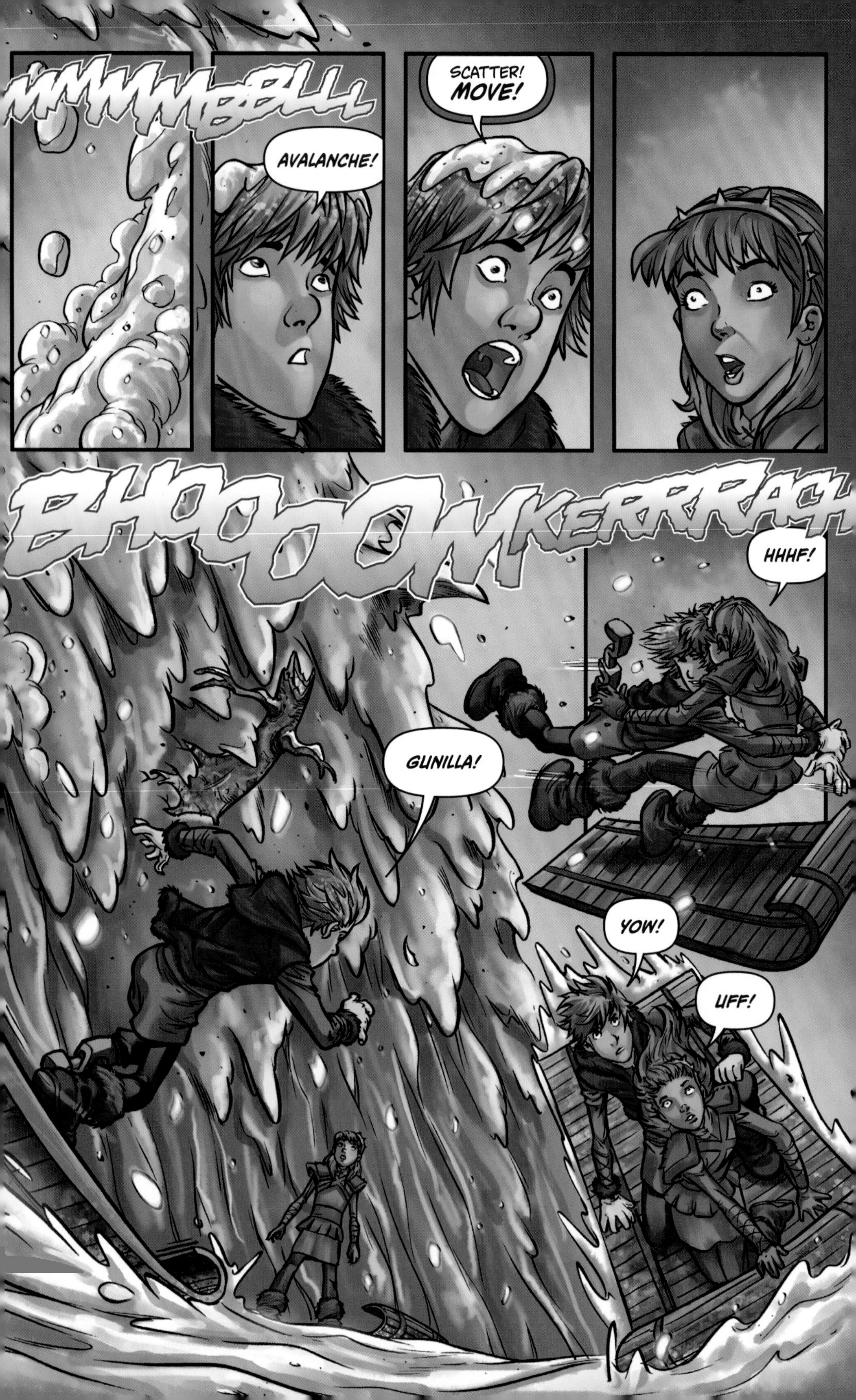
MMMMBLLL
AVALANCHE!
SCATTER!
MOVE!
BHOOOOM
KERRRACH
HHHF!
GUNILLA!
YOW!
UFF!

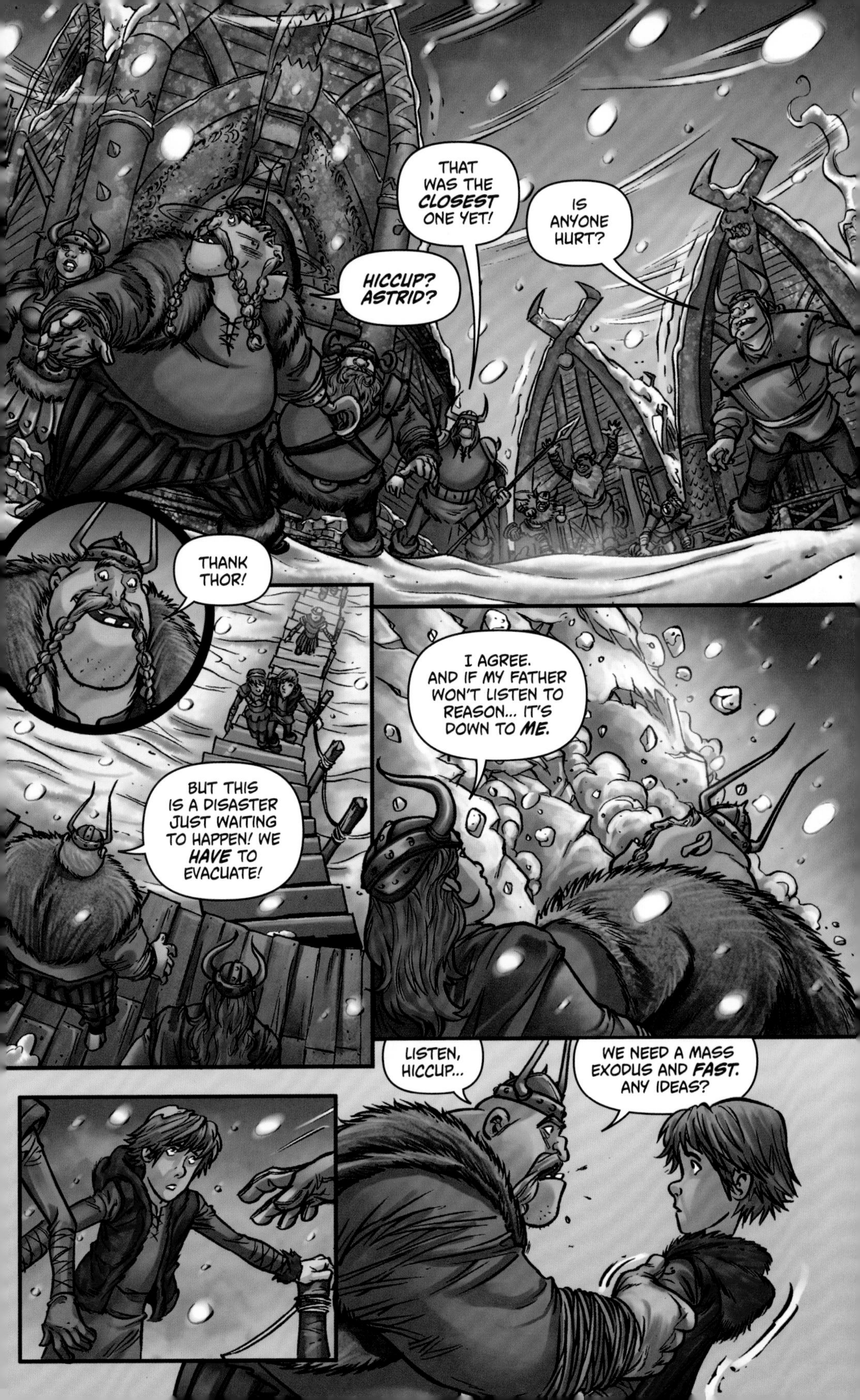
HICCUP? ASTRID?
THAT WAS THE CLOSEST ONE YET!
IS ANYONE HURT?
THANK THOR!
BUT THIS IS A DISASTER JUST WAITING TO HAPPEN! WE HAVE TO EVACUATE!
I AGREE. AND IF MY FATHER WON'T LISTEN TO REASON... IT'S DOWN TO ME.
LISTEN, HICCUP...
WE NEED A MASS EXODUS AND FAST. ANY IDEAS?

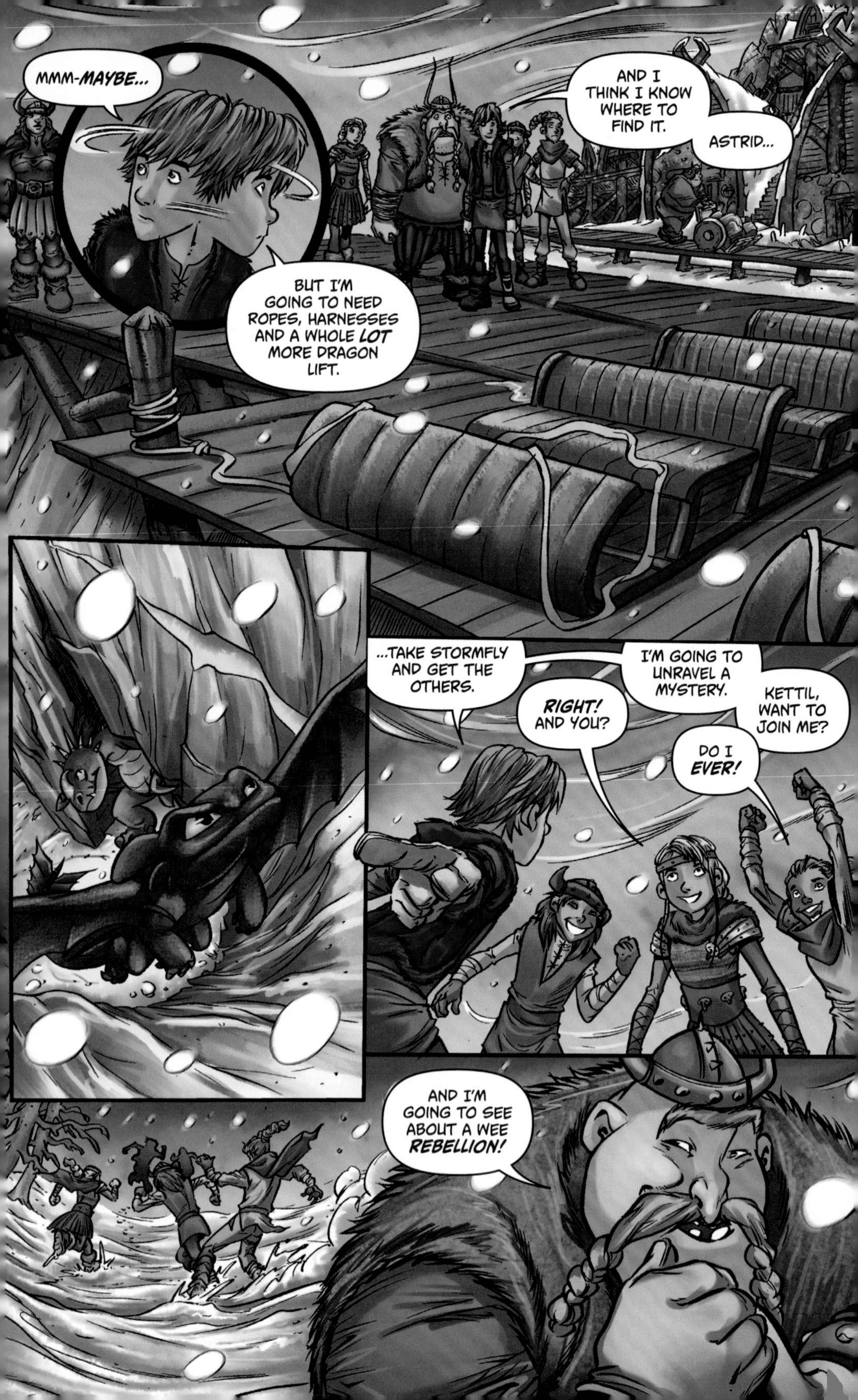
MMM-*MAYBE*...
BUT I'M GOING TO NEED ROPES, HARNESSES AND A WHOLE *LOT* MORE DRAGON LIFT.
AND I THINK I KNOW WHERE TO FIND IT.
ASTRID...
...TAKE STORMFLY AND GET THE OTHERS.
RIGHT! AND YOU?
I'M GOING TO UNRAVEL A MYSTERY.
KETTIL, WANT TO JOIN ME?
DO I *EVER!*
AND I'M GOING TO SEE ABOUT A WEE *REBELLION!*

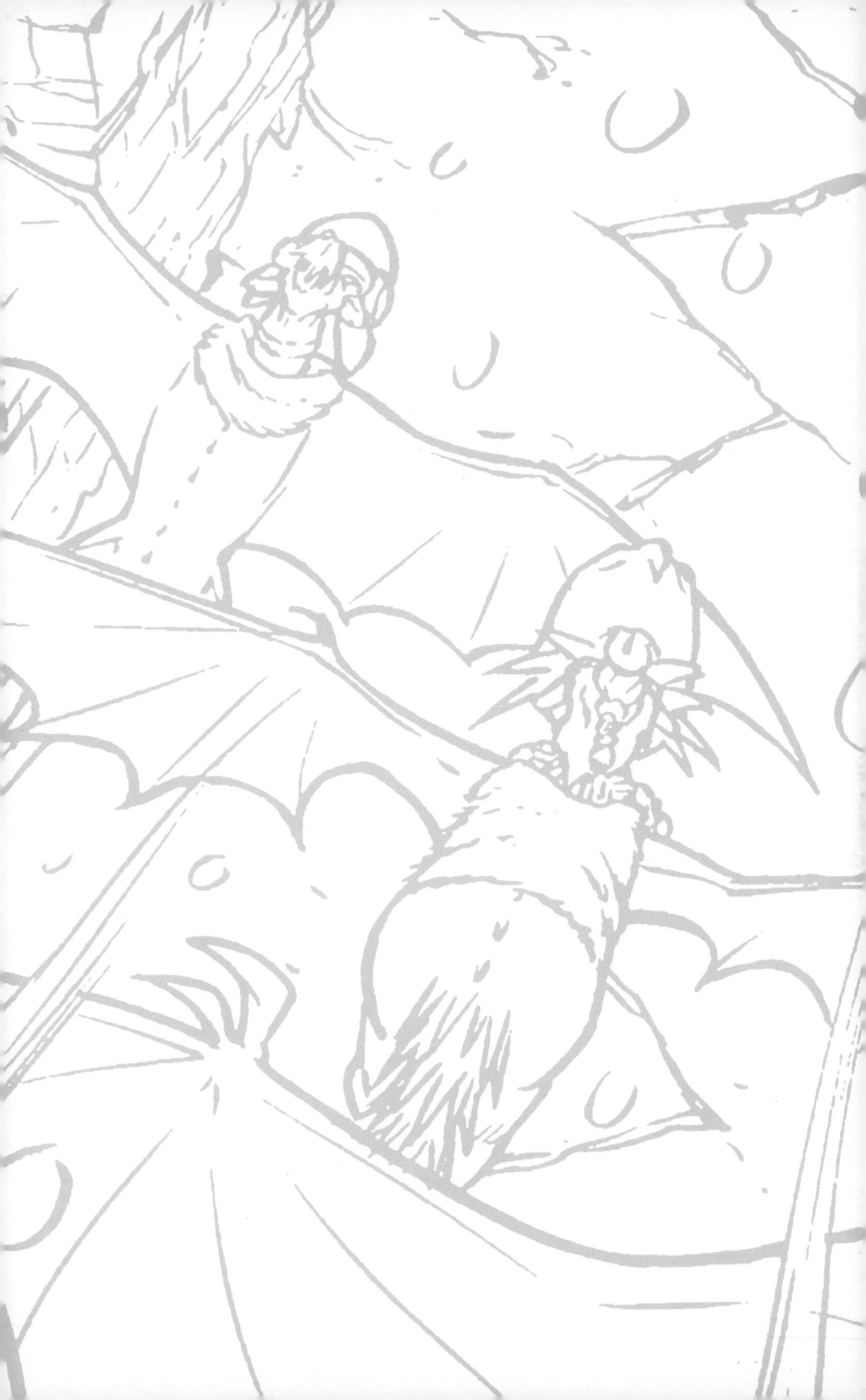

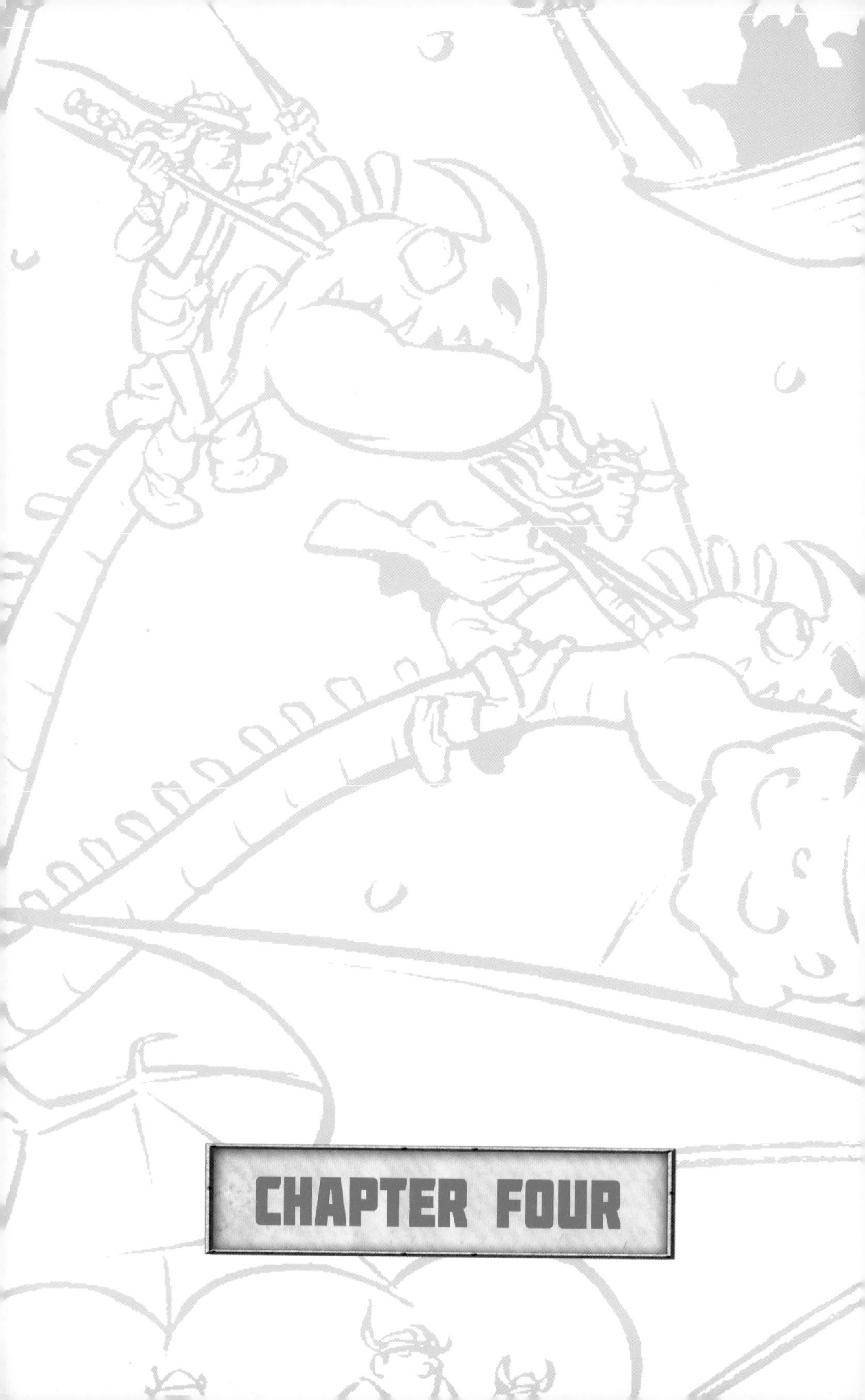

CHAPTER FOUR

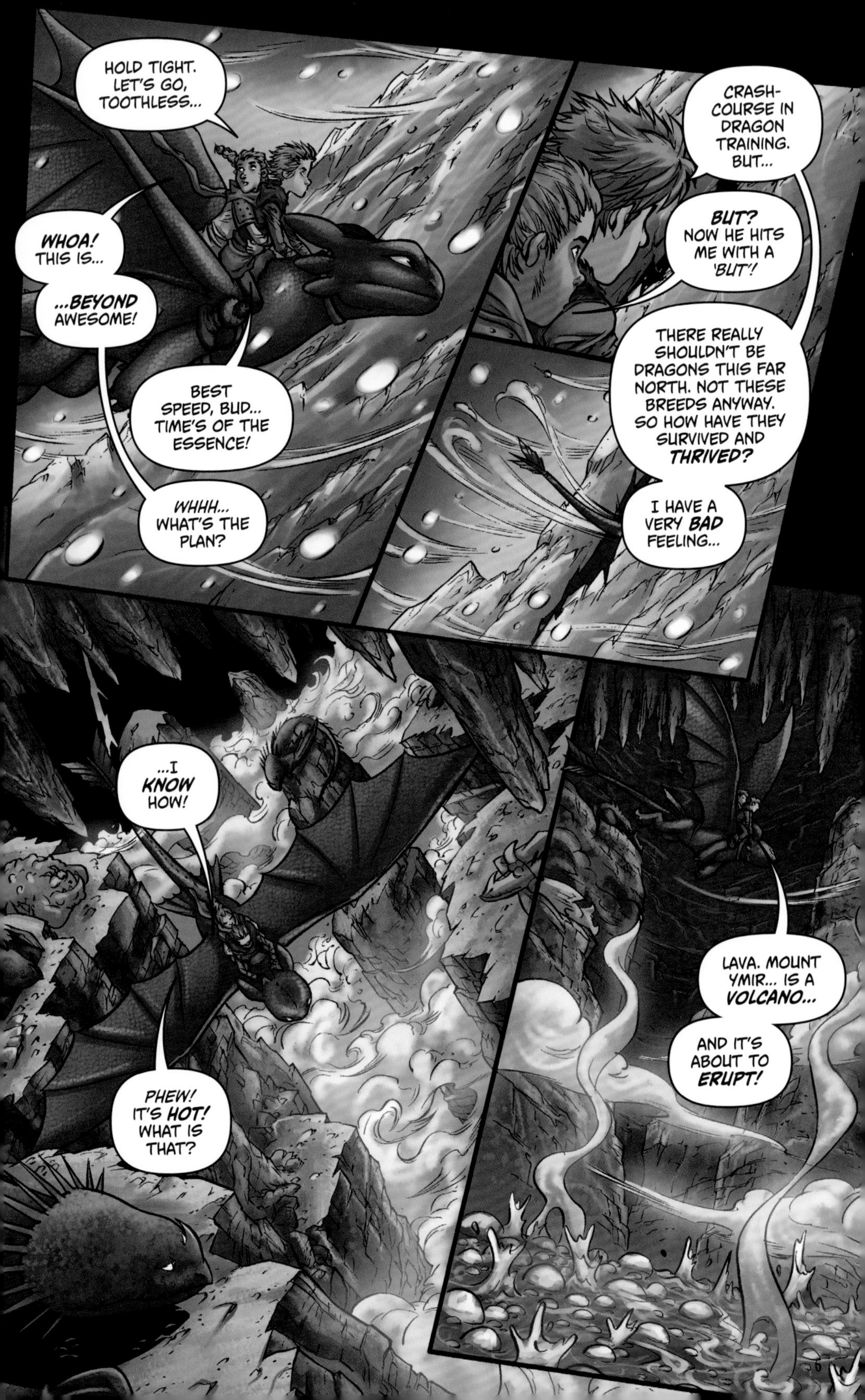
HOLD TIGHT. LET'S GO, TOOTHLESS...
WHOA! THIS IS...
...BEYOND AWESOME!
BEST SPEED, BUD... TIME'S OF THE ESSENCE!
WHHH... WHAT'S THE PLAN?
CRASH-COURSE IN DRAGON TRAINING. BUT...
BUT? NOW HE HITS ME WITH A 'BUT'!
THERE REALLY SHOULDN'T BE DRAGONS THIS FAR NORTH. NOT THESE BREEDS ANYWAY. SO HOW HAVE THEY SURVIVED AND THRIVED?
I HAVE A VERY BAD FEELING...
...I KNOW HOW!
PHEW! IT'S HOT! WHAT IS THAT?
LAVA. MOUNT YMIR... IS A VOLCANO...
AND IT'S ABOUT TO ERUPT!

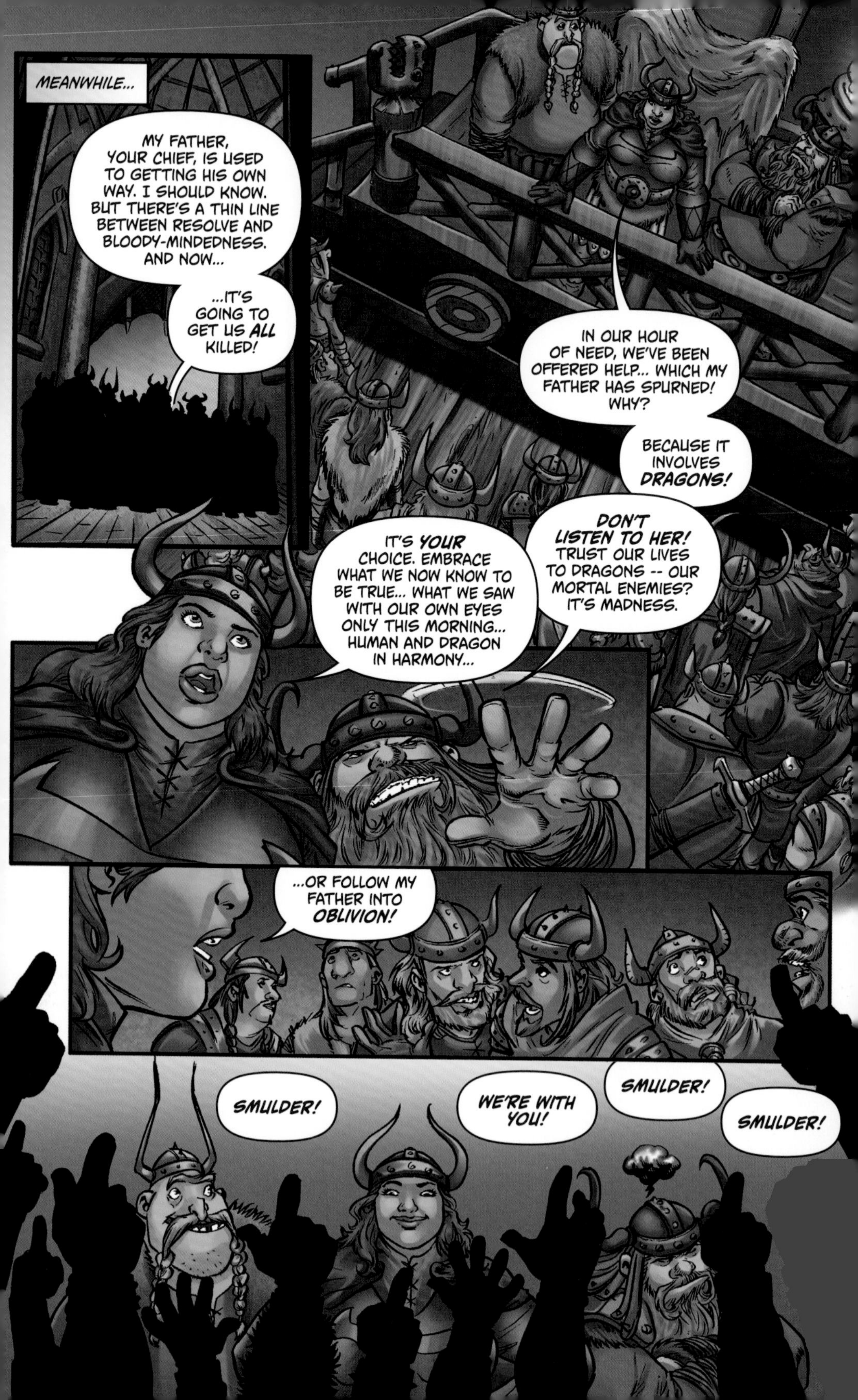
MEANWHILE...
MY FATHER, YOUR CHIEF, IS USED TO GETTING HIS OWN WAY. I SHOULD KNOW. BUT THERE'S A THIN LINE BETWEEN RESOLVE AND BLOODY-MINDEDNESS. AND NOW...
...IT'S GOING TO GET US ALL KILLED!
IN OUR HOUR OF NEED, WE'VE BEEN OFFERED HELP... WHICH MY FATHER HAS SPURNED! WHY?
BECAUSE IT INVOLVES DRAGONS!
IT'S YOUR CHOICE. EMBRACE WHAT WE NOW KNOW TO BE TRUE... WHAT WE SAW WITH OUR OWN EYES ONLY THIS MORNING... HUMAN AND DRAGON IN HARMONY...
DON'T LISTEN TO HER! TRUST OUR LIVES TO DRAGONS -- OUR MORTAL ENEMIES? IT'S MADNESS.
...OR FOLLOW MY FATHER INTO OBLIVION!
SMULDER!
WE'RE WITH YOU!
SMULDER!
SMULDER!

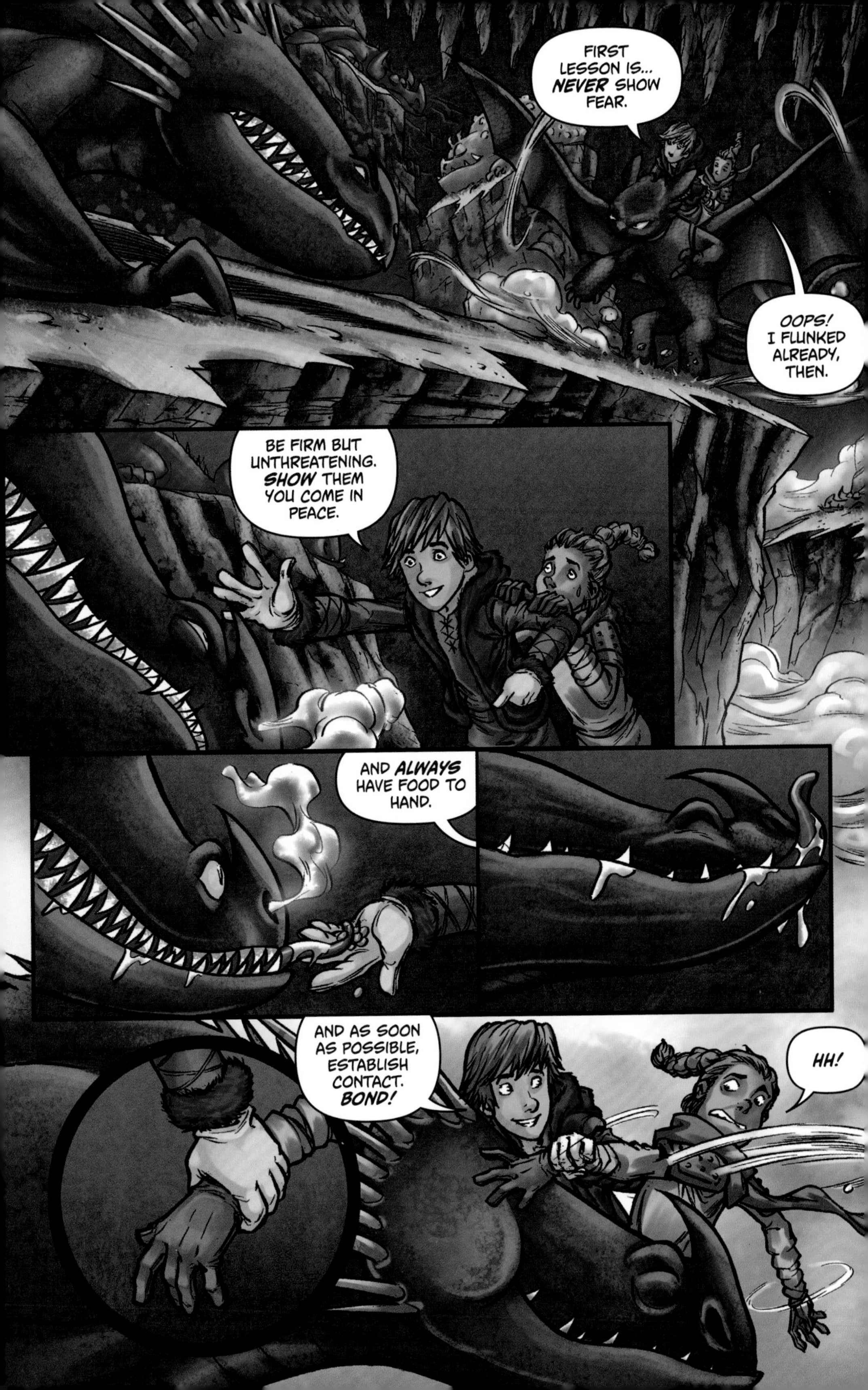
FIRST LESSON IS... NEVER SHOW FEAR.
OOPS! I FLUNKED ALREADY, THEN.
BE FIRM BUT UNTHREATENING. SHOW THEM YOU COME IN PEACE.
AND ALWAYS HAVE FOOD TO HAND.
AND AS SOON AS POSSIBLE, ESTABLISH CONTACT. BOND!
HH!

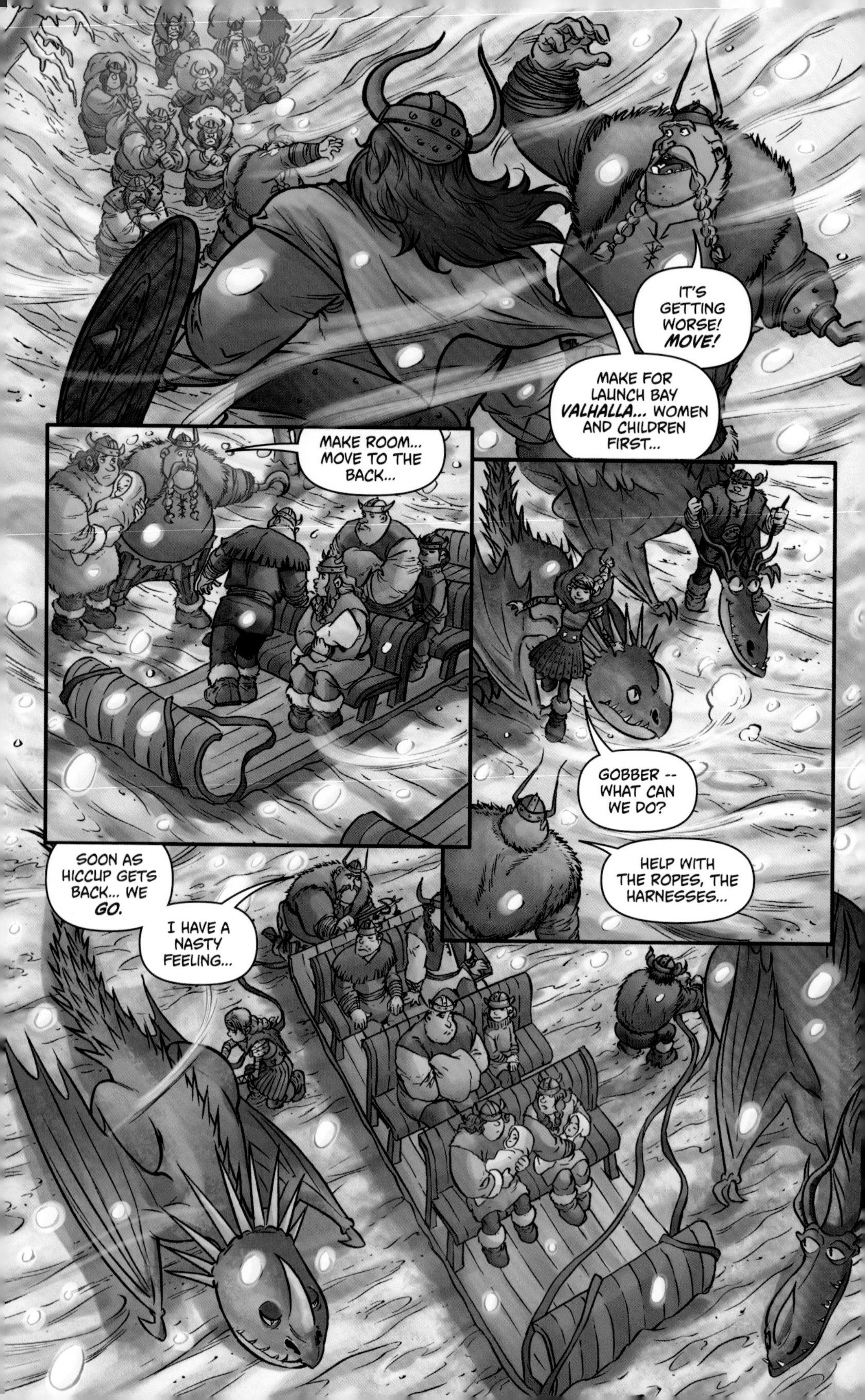
IT'S GETTING WORSE! *MOVE!*
MAKE FOR LAUNCH BAY *VALHALLA...* WOMEN AND CHILDREN FIRST...
MAKE ROOM... MOVE TO THE BACK...
GOBBER -- WHAT CAN WE DO?
HELP WITH THE ROPES, THE HARNESSES...
SOON AS HICCUP GETS BACK... WE *GO.*
I HAVE A NASTY FEELING...

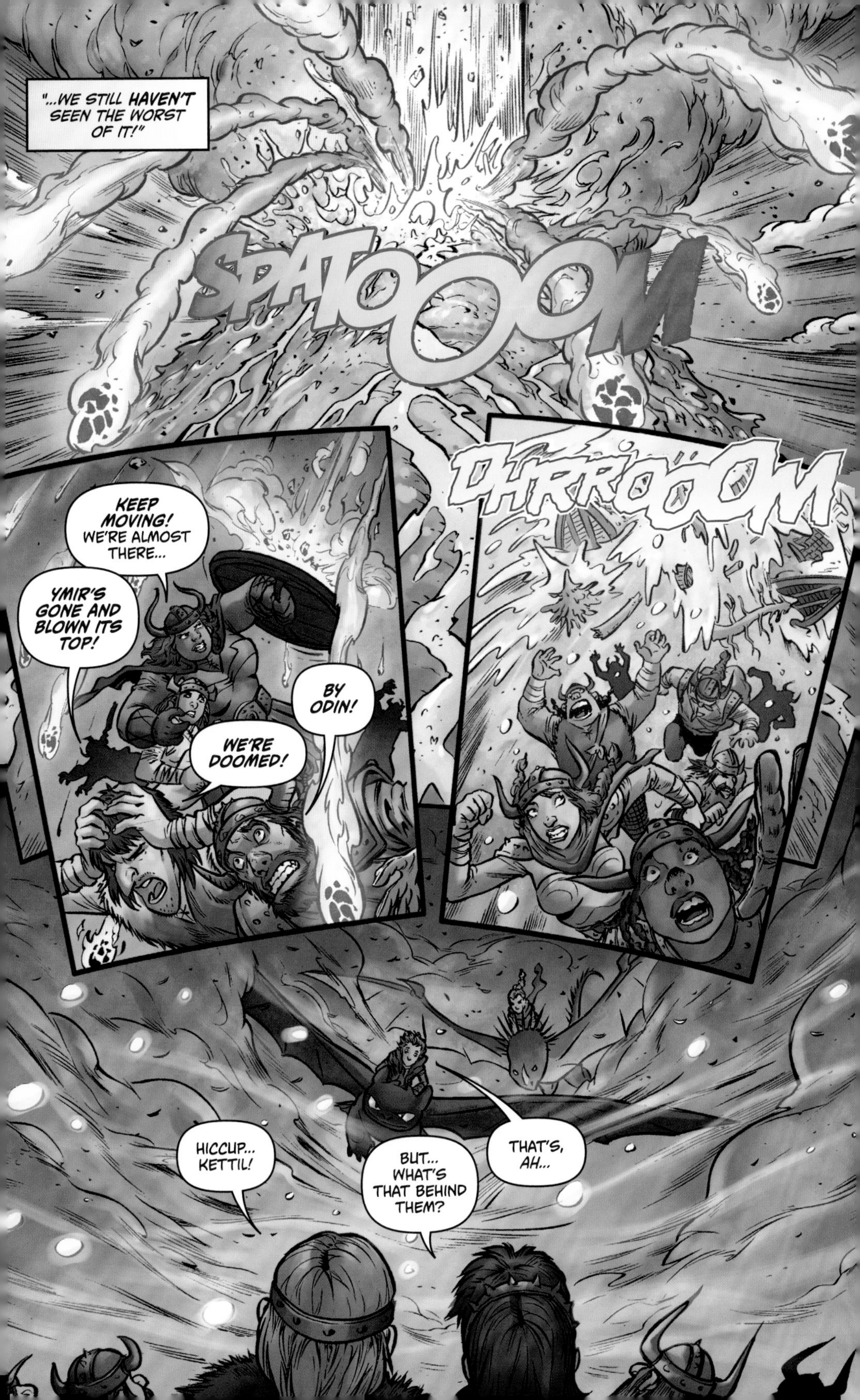
"...WE STILL HAVEN'T SEEN THE WORST OF IT!"
SPATOOOM
KEEP MOVING! WE'RE ALMOST THERE...
YMIR'S GONE AND BLOWN ITS TOP!
BY ODIN!
WE'RE DOOMED!
DHRROOOM
HICCUP... KETTIL!
BUT... WHAT'S THAT BEHIND THEM?
THAT'S, AH...

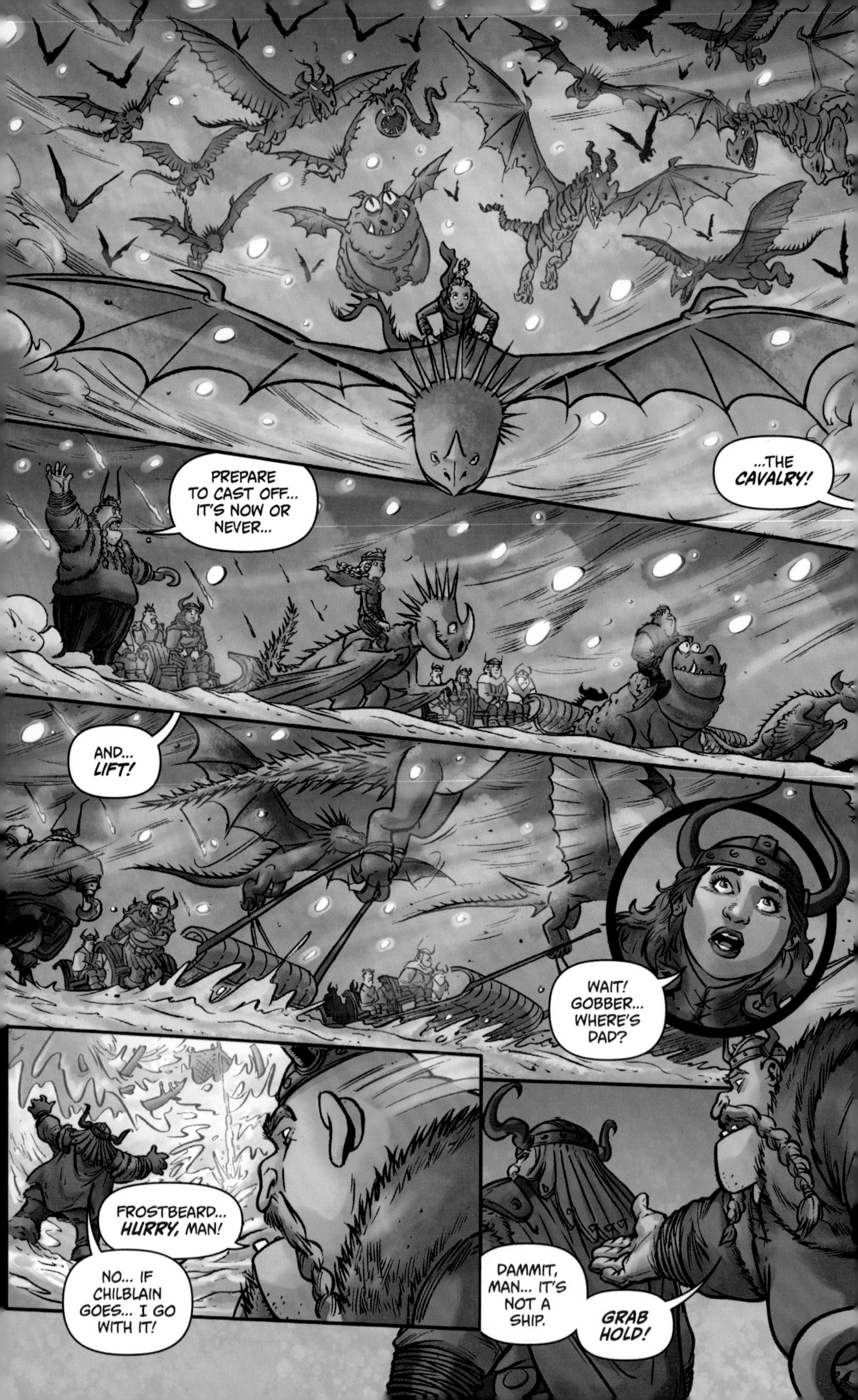
...THE CAVALRY!
PREPARE TO CAST OFF... IT'S NOW OR NEVER...
AND... LIFT!
WAIT! GOBBER... WHERE'S DAD?
FROSTBEARD... HURRY, MAN!
NO... IF CHILBLAIN GOES... I GO WITH IT!
DAMMIT, MAN... IT'S NOT A SHIP.
GRAB HOLD!

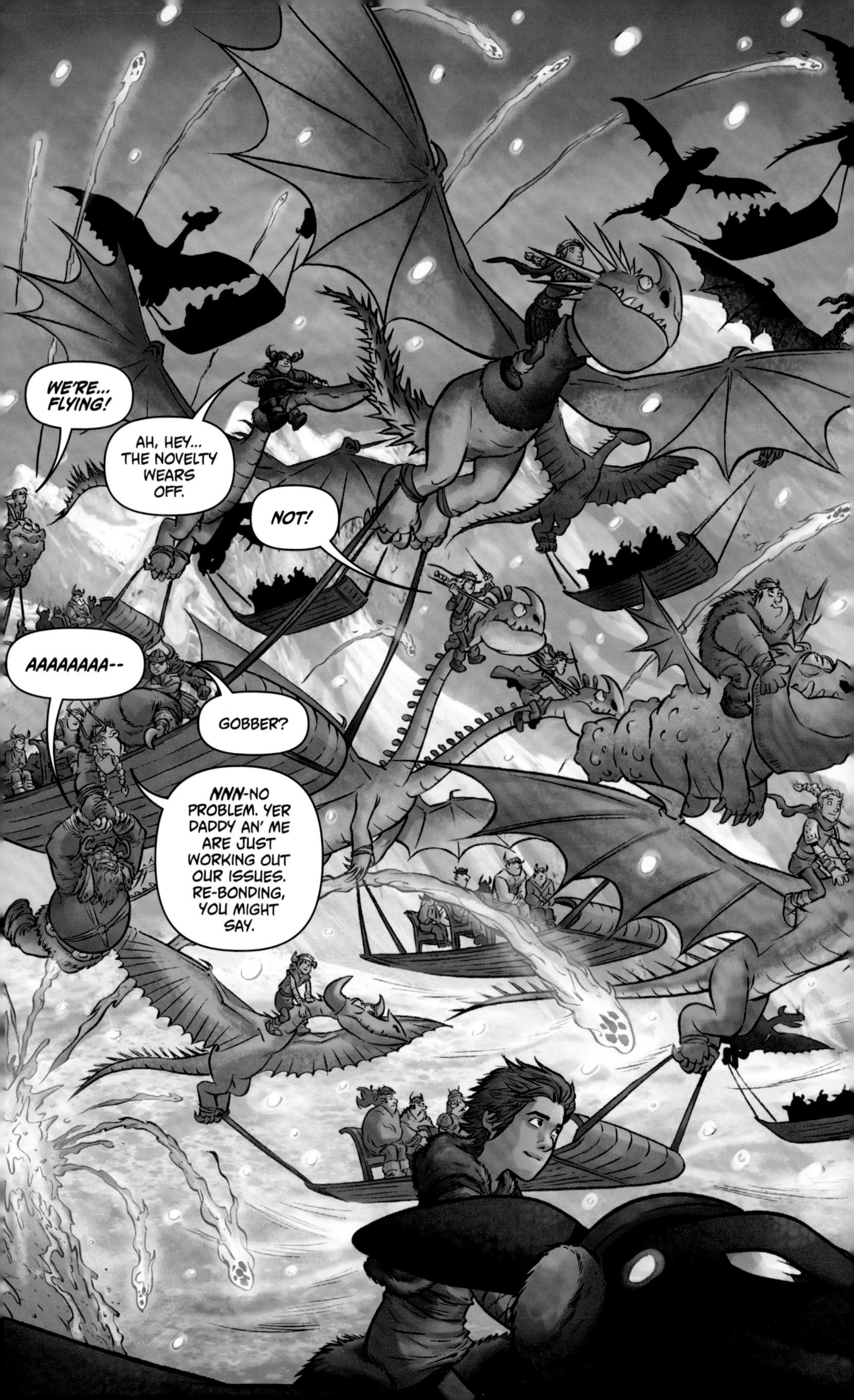
WE'RE... FLYING!
AH, HEY... THE NOVELTY WEARS OFF.
NOT!
AAAAAAAA--
GOBBER?
NNN-NO PROBLEM. YER DADDY AN' ME ARE JUST WORKING OUT OUR ISSUES. RE-BONDING, YOU MIGHT SAY.

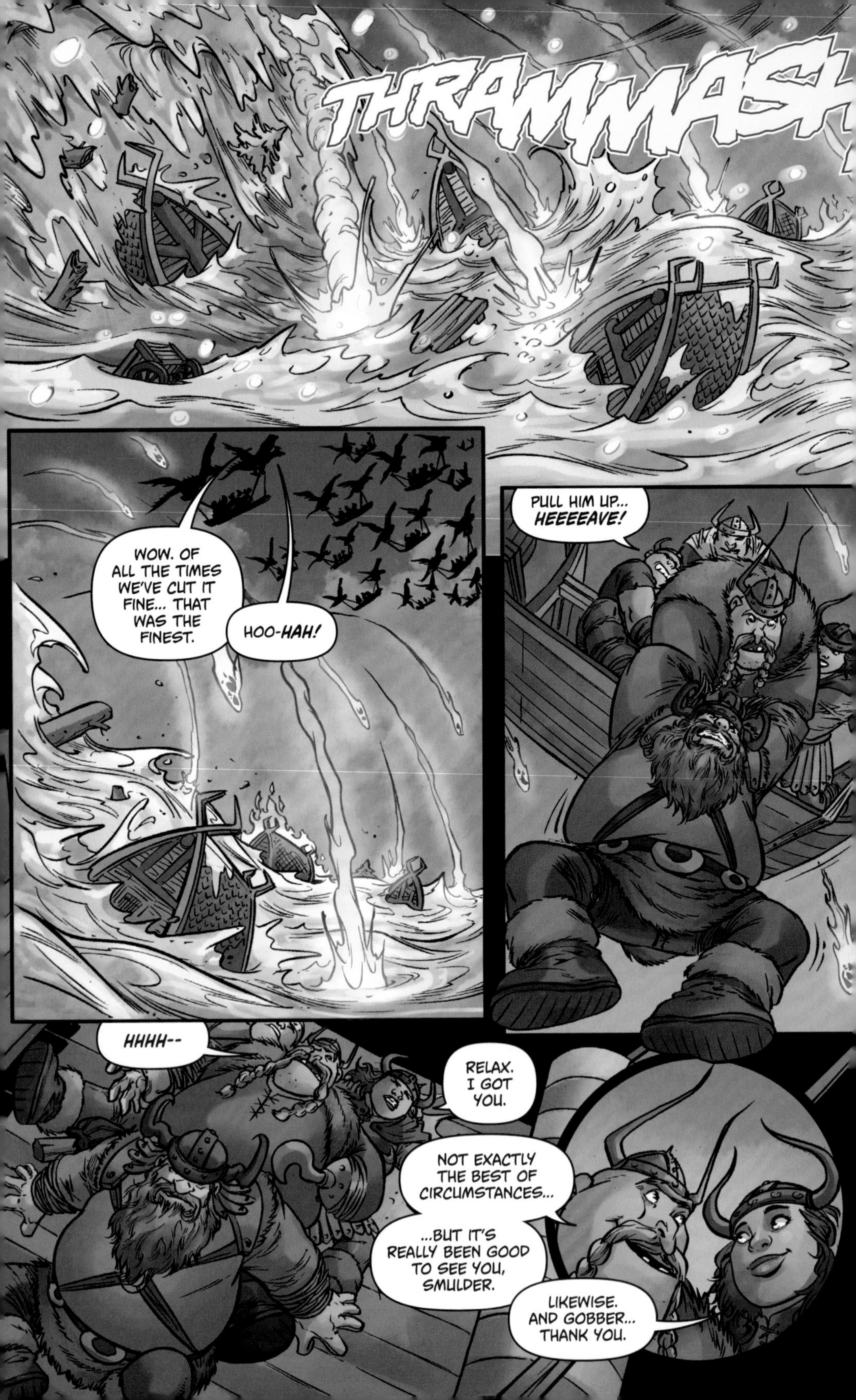
THRAMMASH
WOW. OF ALL THE TIMES WE'VE CUT IT FINE... THAT WAS THE FINEST.
HOO-HAH!
PULL HIM UP... HEEEEAVE!
HHHH--
RELAX. I GOT YOU.
NOT EXACTLY THE BEST OF CIRCUMSTANCES...
...BUT IT'S REALLY BEEN GOOD TO SEE YOU, SMULDER.
LIKEWISE. AND GOBBER... THANK YOU.

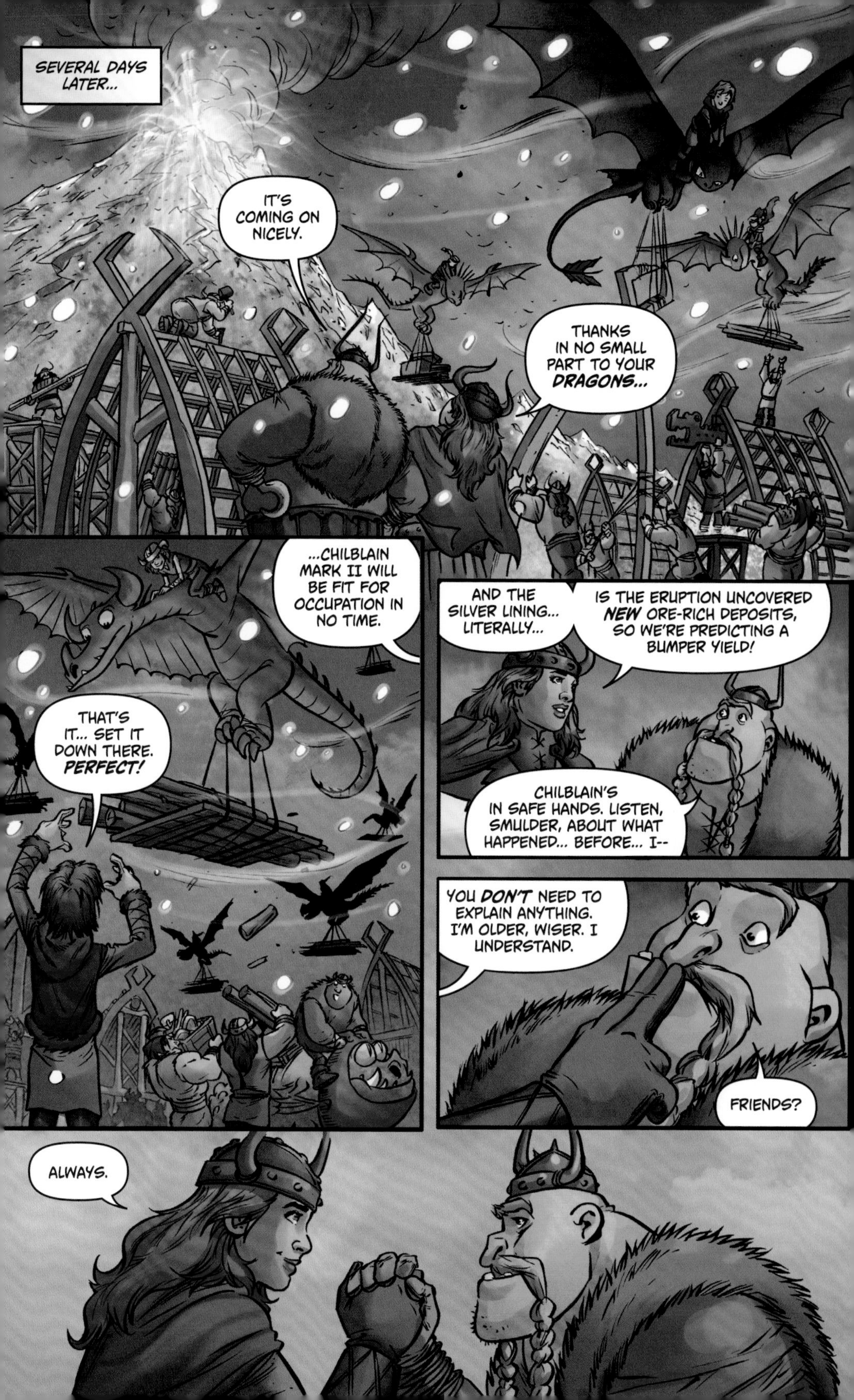
SEVERAL DAYS LATER...
IT'S COMING ON NICELY.
THANKS IN NO SMALL PART TO YOUR DRAGONS...
...CHILBLAIN MARK II WILL BE FIT FOR OCCUPATION IN NO TIME.
THAT'S IT... SET IT DOWN THERE. PERFECT!
AND THE SILVER LINING... LITERALLY...
IS THE ERUPTION UNCOVERED NEW ORE-RICH DEPOSITS, SO WE'RE PREDICTING A BUMPER YIELD!
CHILBLAIN'S IN SAFE HANDS. LISTEN, SMULDER, ABOUT WHAT HAPPENED... BEFORE... I--
YOU DON'T NEED TO EXPLAIN ANYTHING. I'M OLDER, WISER. I UNDERSTAND.
FRIENDS?
ALWAYS.

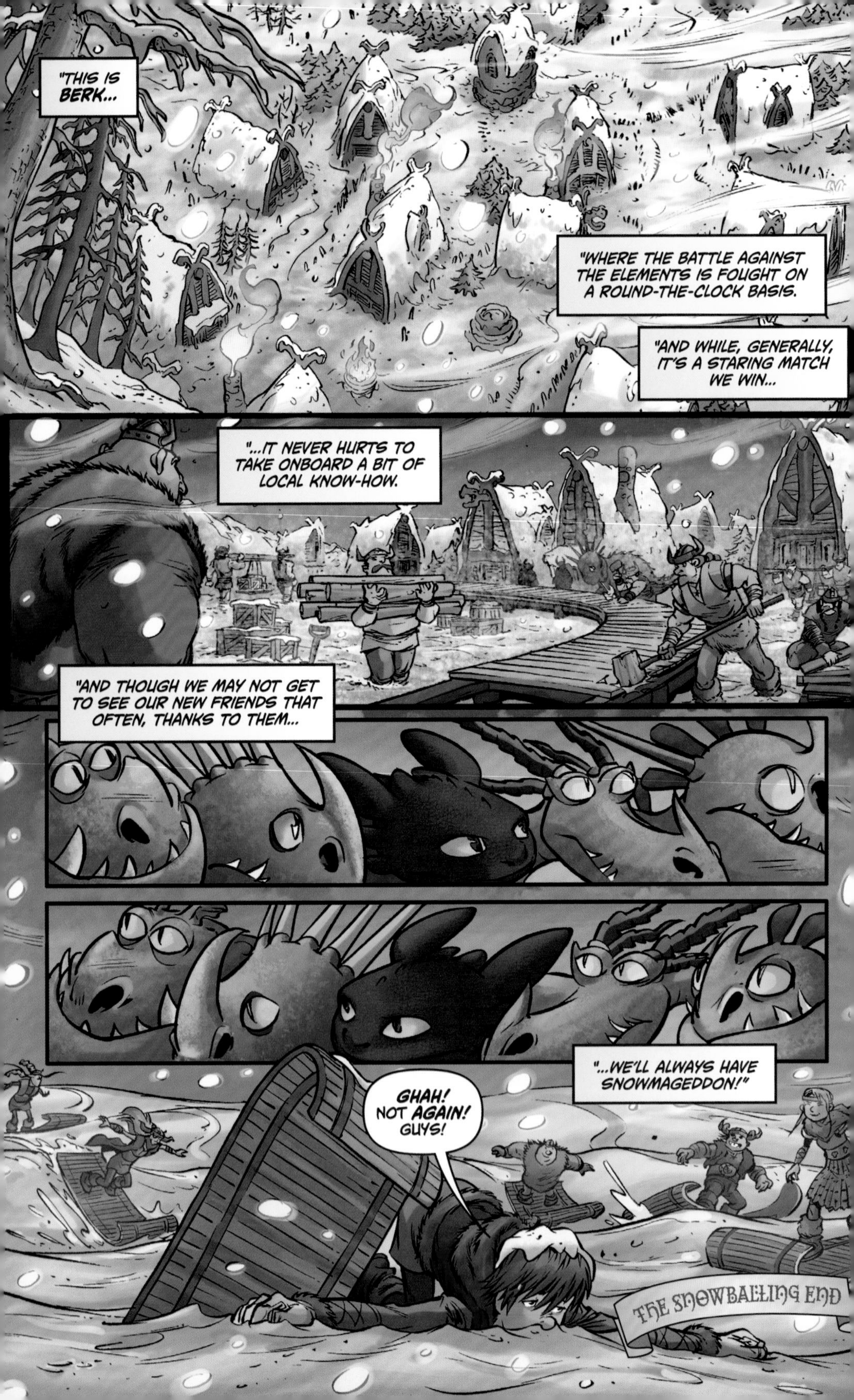
"THIS IS BERK...
"WHERE THE BATTLE AGAINST THE ELEMENTS IS FOUGHT ON A ROUND-THE-CLOCK BASIS.
"AND WHILE, GENERALLY, IT'S A STARING MATCH WE WIN...
"...IT NEVER HURTS TO TAKE ONBOARD A BIT OF LOCAL KNOW-HOW.
"AND THOUGH WE MAY NOT GET TO SEE OUR NEW FRIENDS THAT OFTEN, THANKS TO THEM...
"...WE'LL ALWAYS HAVE SNOWMAGEDDON!"
GHAH! NOT AGAIN! GUYS!
THE SNOWBALLING END

THAW FLEET

SCRIPT
SIMON FURMAN

ARTIST
JACK LAWRENCE

COLORS
DIGIKORE

LETTERING
JIM CAMPBELL

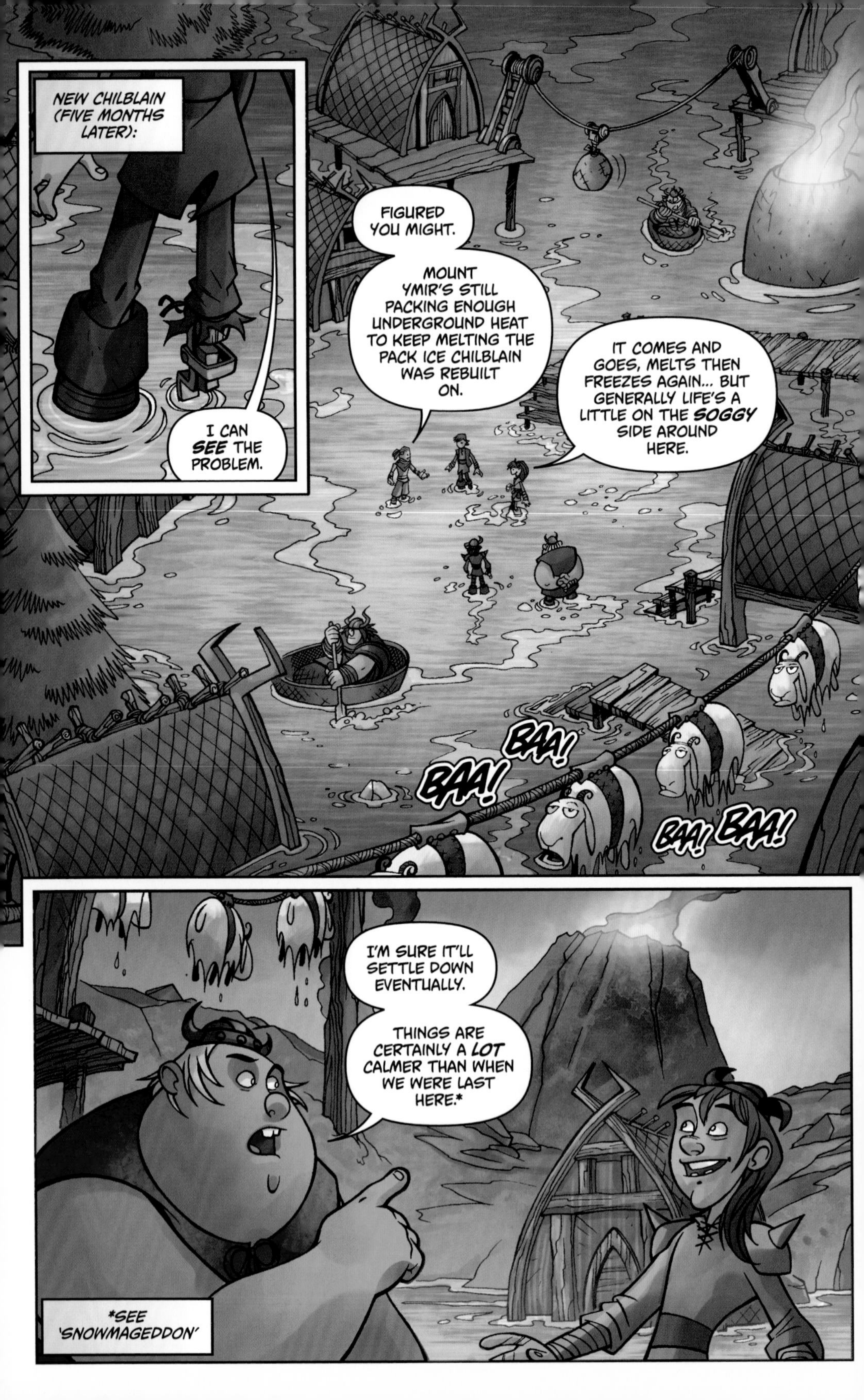
NEW CHILBLAIN (FIVE MONTHS LATER):
I CAN SEE THE PROBLEM.
FIGURED YOU MIGHT.
MOUNT YMIR'S STILL PACKING ENOUGH UNDERGROUND HEAT TO KEEP MELTING THE PACK ICE CHILBLAIN WAS REBUILT ON.
IT COMES AND GOES, MELTS THEN FREEZES AGAIN... BUT GENERALLY LIFE'S A LITTLE ON THE SOGGY SIDE AROUND HERE.
BAA!
BAA!
BAA!
BAA!
I'M SURE IT'LL SETTLE DOWN EVENTUALLY.
THINGS ARE CERTAINLY A LOT CALMER THAN WHEN WE WERE LAST HERE.*
*SEE 'SNOWMAGEDDON'

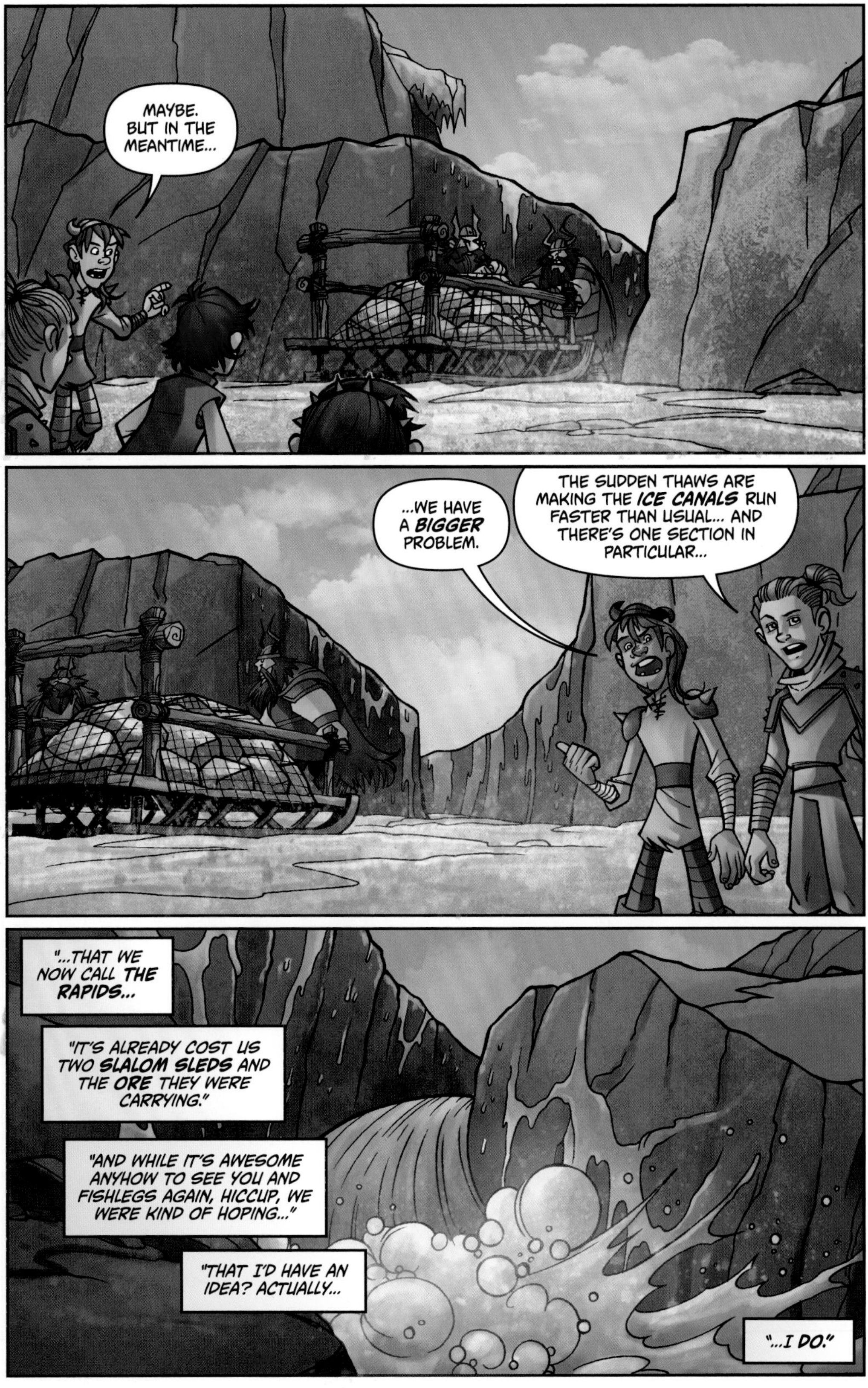
MAYBE. BUT IN THE MEANTIME...
...WE HAVE A **BIGGER** PROBLEM.
THE SUDDEN THAWS ARE MAKING THE ***ICE CANALS*** RUN FASTER THAN USUAL... AND THERE'S ONE SECTION IN PARTICULAR...
*"...THAT WE NOW CALL **THE RAPIDS...***
*"IT'S ALREADY COST US TWO **SLALOM SLEDS** AND THE **ORE** THEY WERE CARRYING."*
"AND WHILE IT'S AWESOME ANYHOW TO SEE YOU AND FISHLEGS AGAIN, HICCUP, WE WERE KIND OF HOPING..."
"THAT I'D HAVE AN IDEA? ACTUALLY...
*"...I **DO**."*

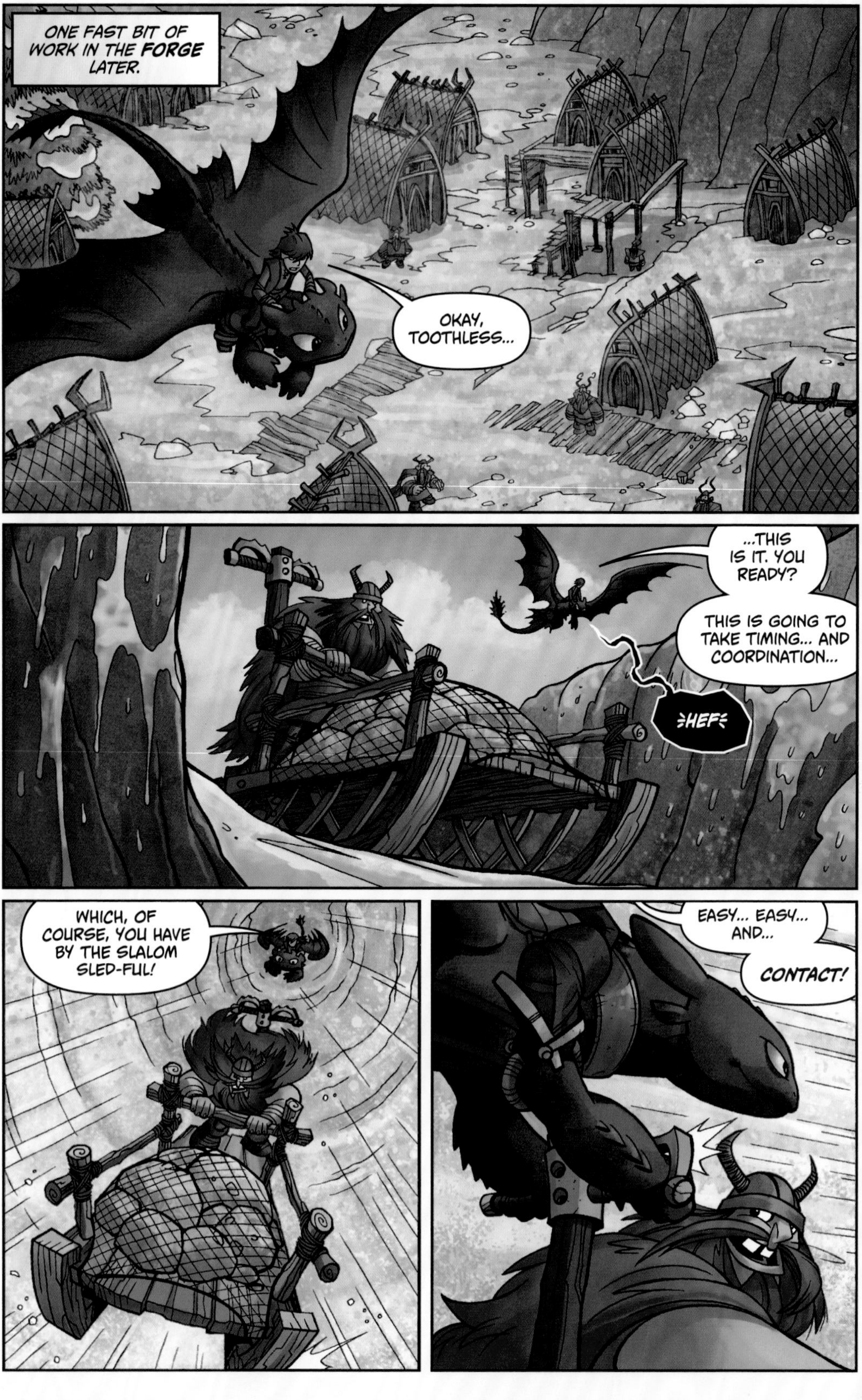
ONE FAST BIT OF WORK IN THE FORGE LATER.
OKAY, TOOTHLESS...
...THIS IS IT. YOU READY?
THIS IS GOING TO TAKE TIMING... AND COORDINATION...
HEF
WHICH, OF COURSE, YOU HAVE BY THE SLALOM SLED-FUL!
EASY... EASY... AND...
CONTACT!

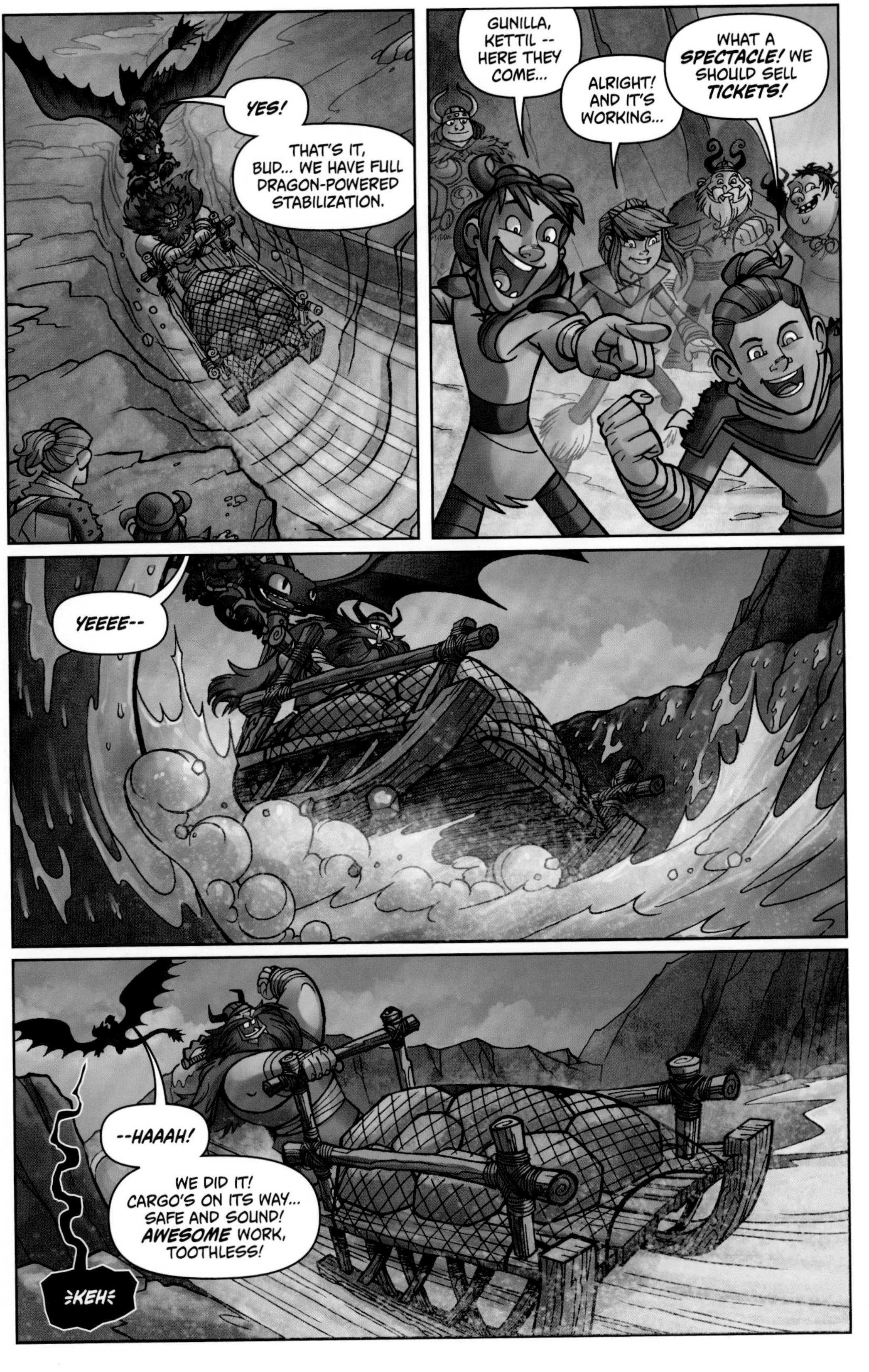
YES!
THAT'S IT, BUD... WE HAVE FULL DRAGON-POWERED STABILIZATION.
GUNILLA, KETTIL -- HERE THEY COME...
ALRIGHT! AND IT'S WORKING...
WHAT A SPECTACLE! WE SHOULD SELL TICKETS!
YEEEE--
--HAAAH!
WE DID IT! CARGO'S ON ITS WAY... SAFE AND SOUND! AWESOME WORK, TOOTHLESS!
KEH

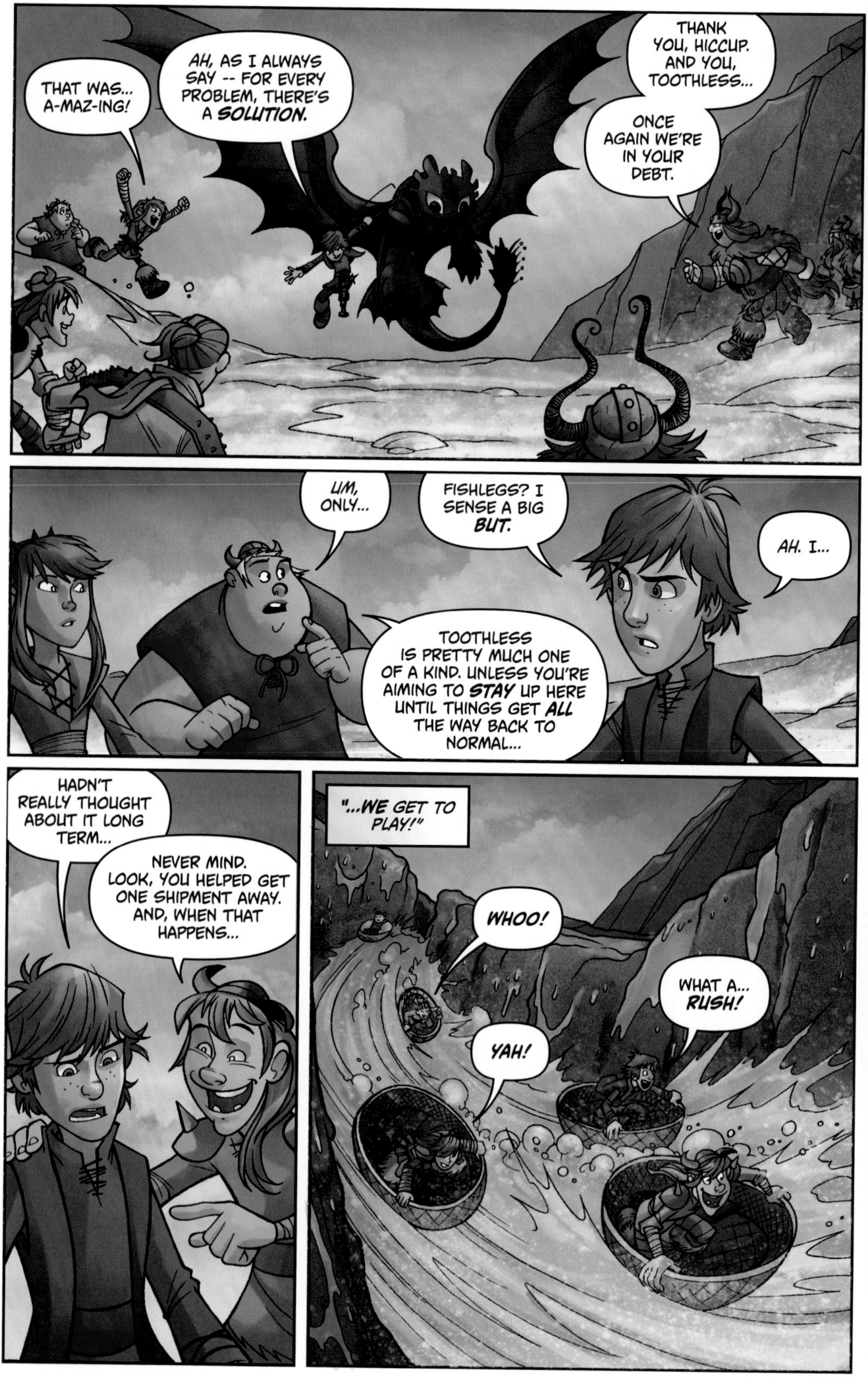
THAT WAS... A-MAZ-ING!
AH, AS I ALWAYS SAY -- FOR EVERY PROBLEM, THERE'S A SOLUTION.
THANK YOU, HICCUP. AND YOU, TOOTHLESS...
ONCE AGAIN WE'RE IN YOUR DEBT.
UM, ONLY...
FISHLEGS? I SENSE A BIG BUT.
AH. I...
TOOTHLESS IS PRETTY MUCH ONE OF A KIND. UNLESS YOU'RE AIMING TO STAY UP HERE UNTIL THINGS GET ALL THE WAY BACK TO NORMAL...
HADN'T REALLY THOUGHT ABOUT IT LONG TERM...
NEVER MIND. LOOK, YOU HELPED GET ONE SHIPMENT AWAY. AND, WHEN THAT HAPPENS...
"...WE GET TO PLAY!"
WHOO!
WHAT A... RUSH!
YAH!

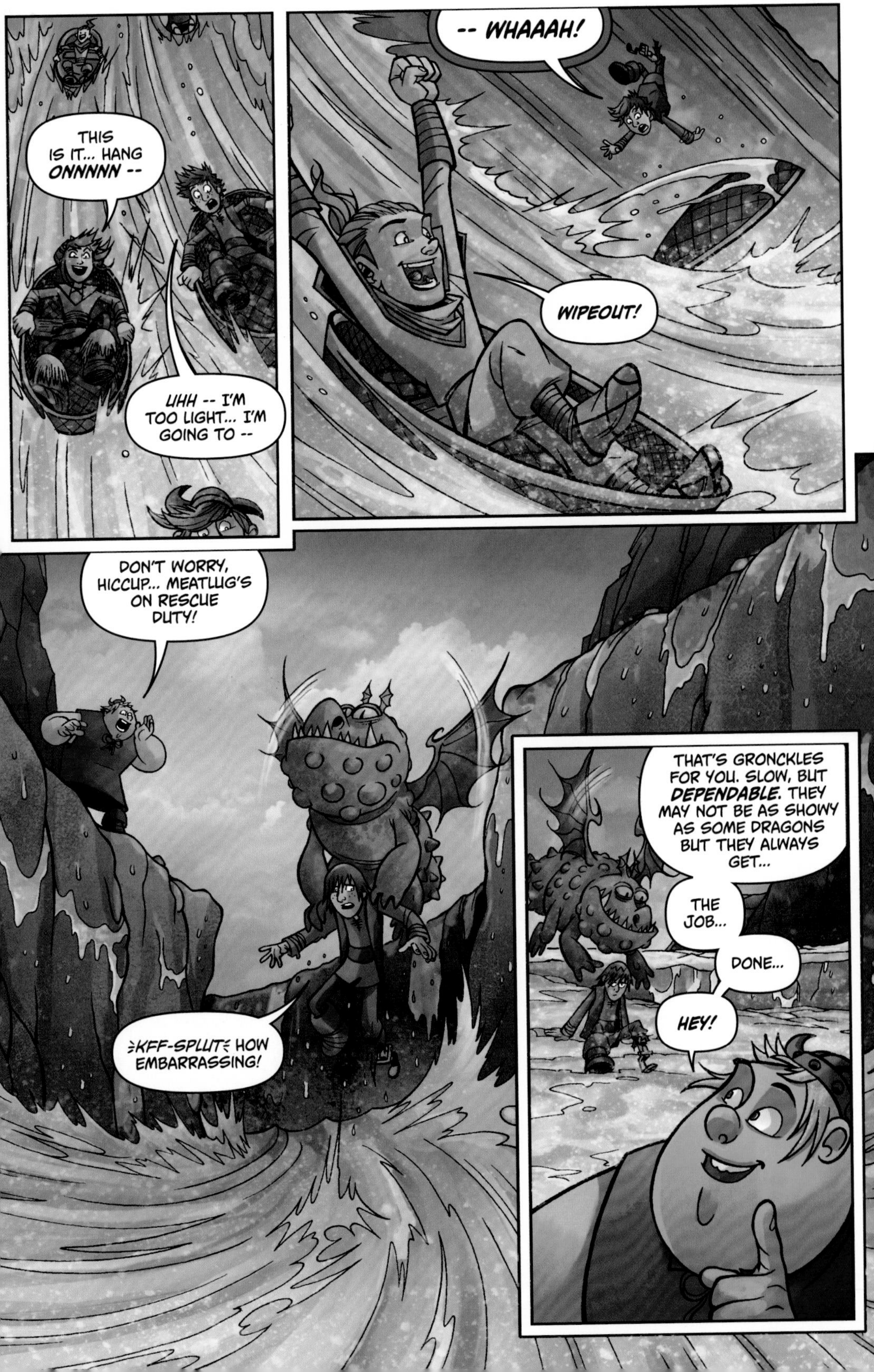
THIS IS IT... HANG ONNNNN --
UHH -- I'M TOO LIGHT... I'M GOING TO --
-- WHAAAH!
WIPEOUT!
DON'T WORRY, HICCUP... MEATLUG'S ON RESCUE DUTY!
KFF-SPLUT HOW EMBARRASSING!
THAT'S GRONCKLES FOR YOU. SLOW, BUT DEPENDABLE. THEY MAY NOT BE AS SHOWY AS SOME DRAGONS BUT THEY ALWAYS GET...
THE JOB...
DONE...
HEY!

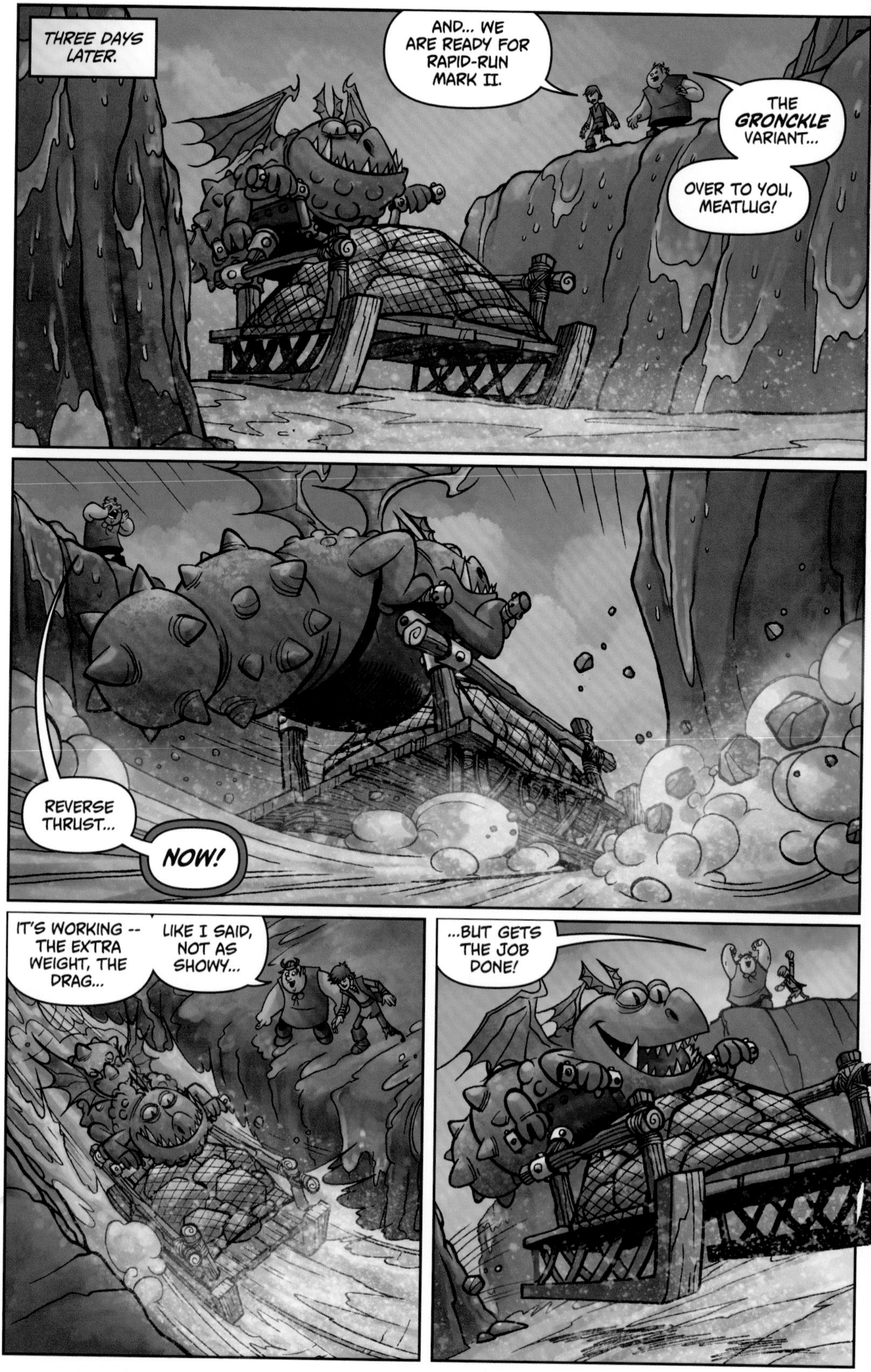
THREE DAYS LATER.
AND... WE ARE READY FOR RAPID-RUN MARK II.
THE GRONCKLE VARIANT...
OVER TO YOU, MEATLUG!
REVERSE THRUST...
NOW!
IT'S WORKING -- THE EXTRA WEIGHT, THE DRAG...
LIKE I SAID, NOT AS SHOWY...
...BUT GETS THE JOB DONE!

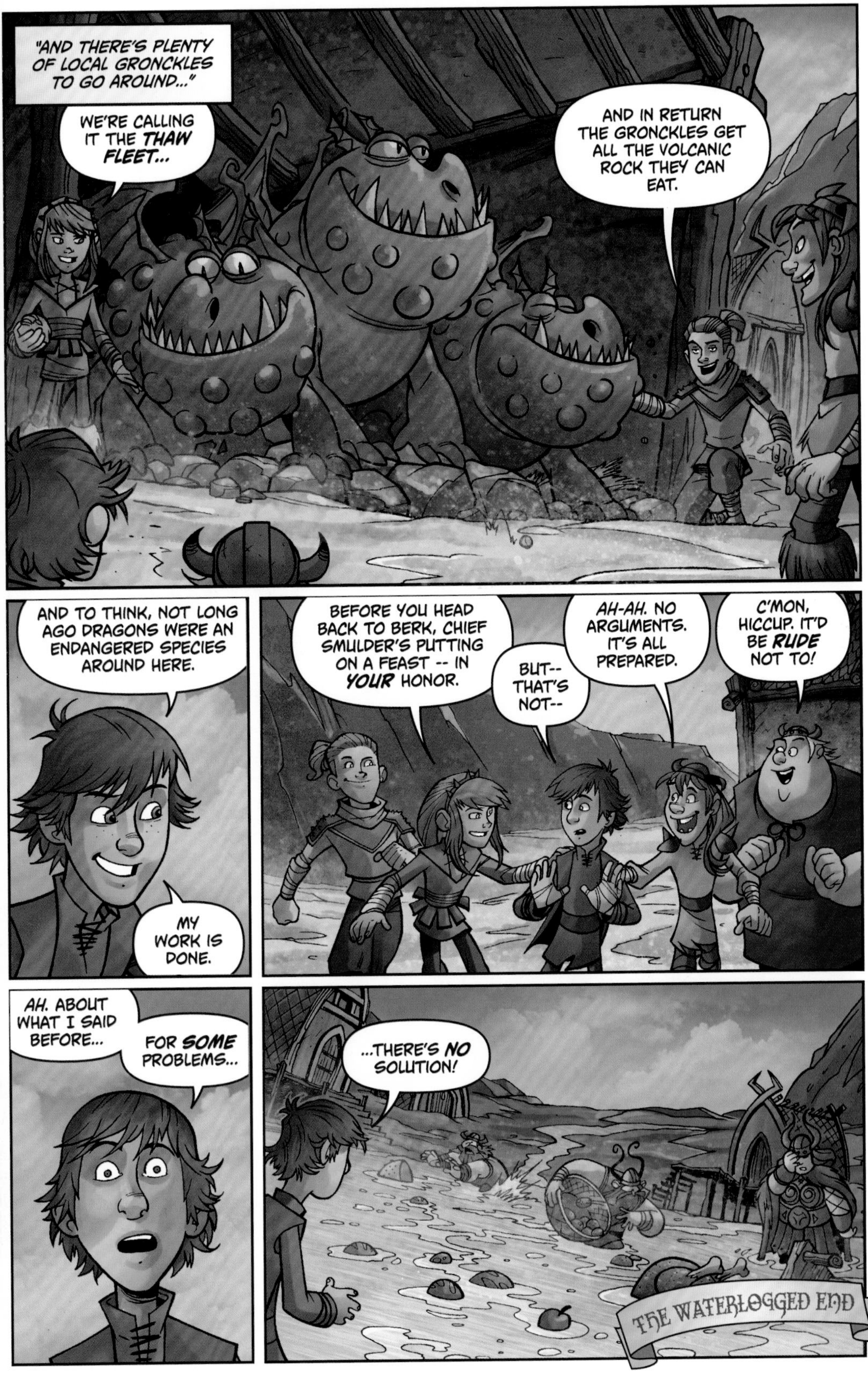
"AND THERE'S PLENTY OF LOCAL GRONCKLES TO GO AROUND..."
WE'RE CALLING IT THE *THAW FLEET*...
AND IN RETURN THE GRONCKLES GET ALL THE VOLCANIC ROCK THEY CAN EAT.
AND TO THINK, NOT LONG AGO DRAGONS WERE AN ENDANGERED SPECIES AROUND HERE.
MY WORK IS DONE.
BEFORE YOU HEAD BACK TO BERK, CHIEF SMULDER'S PUTTING ON A FEAST -- IN *YOUR* HONOR.
BUT-- THAT'S NOT--
AH-AH. NO ARGUMENTS. IT'S ALL PREPARED.
C'MON, HICCUP. IT'D BE *RUDE* NOT TO!
AH. ABOUT WHAT I SAID BEFORE...
FOR *SOME* PROBLEMS...
...THERE'S *NO* SOLUTION!
THE WATERLOGGED END

TITAN COMICS DIGESTS

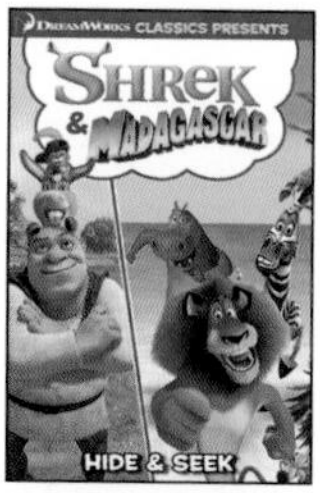
DreamWorks CLASSICS PRESENTS
SHREK & MADAGASCAR
HIDE & SEEK

Dreamworks Classics – 'Hide & Seek'

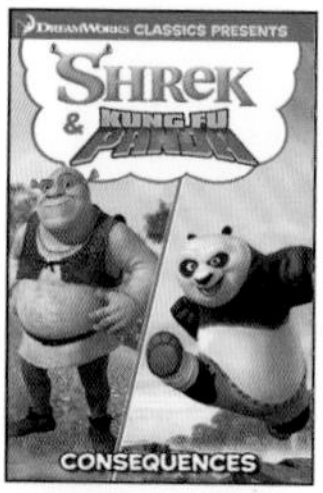
DreamWorks CLASSICS PRESENTS
SHREK & KUNG FU PANDA
CONSEQUENCES

Dreamworks Classics – 'Consequences'

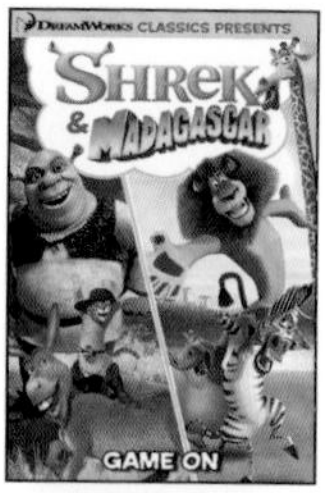
DreamWorks CLASSICS PRESENTS
SHREK & MADAGASCAR
GAME ON

Dreamworks Classics – 'Game On'

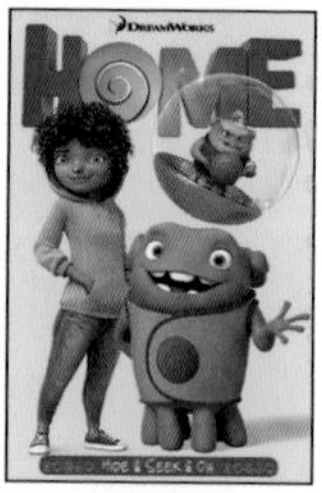
DreamWorks
HOME

Home – Hide & Seek & Oh

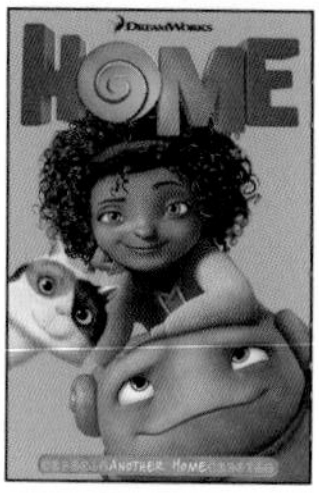
DreamWorks
HOME

Home – Another Home

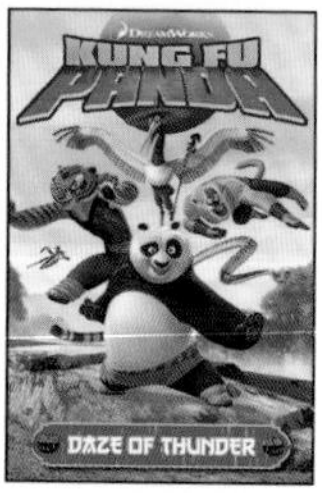
DreamWorks
KUNG FU PANDA
DAZE OF THUNDER

Kung Fu Panda – Daze of Thunder

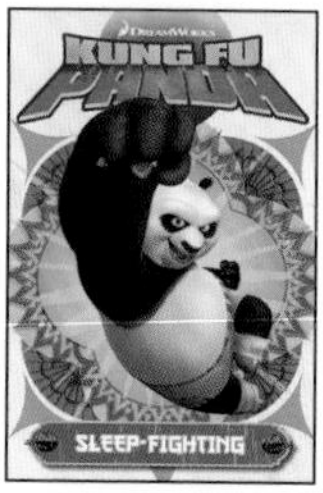
DreamWorks
KUNG FU PANDA
SLEEP-FIGHTING

Kung Fu Panda – Sleep-Fighting

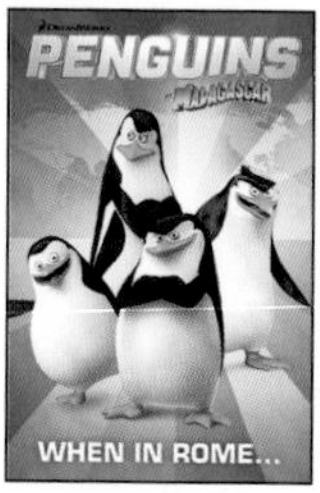
PENGUINS
WHEN IN ROME...

Penguins of Madagascar – When in Rome...

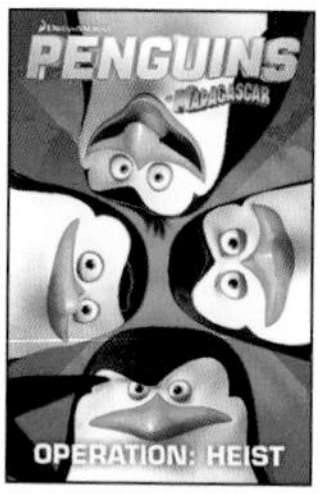
PENGUINS
OPERATION: HEIST

Penguins of Madagascar – Operation: Heist

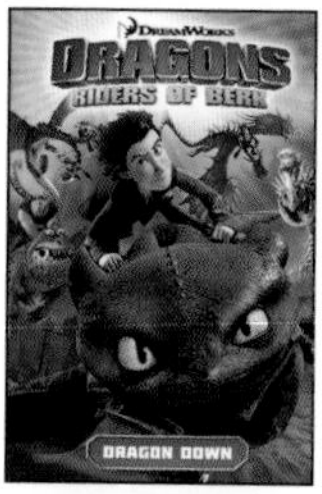
DreamWorks
DRAGONS
RIDERS OF BERK
DRAGON DOWN

DreamWorks Dragons: Riders of Berk – Dragon Down

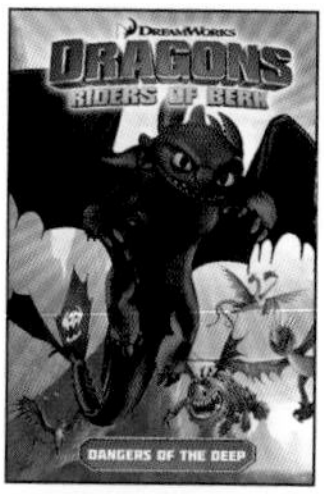
DreamWorks
DRAGONS
RIDERS OF BERK
DANGERS OF THE DEEP

DreamWorks Dragons: Riders of Berk – Dangers of the Deep

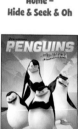

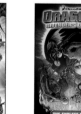

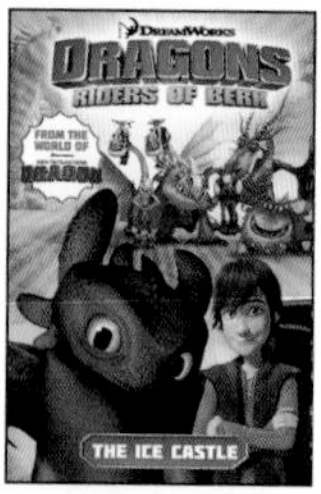
DreamWorks
DRAGONS
RIDERS OF BERK
THE ICE CASTLE

DreamWorks Dragons: Riders of Berk – The Ice Castle

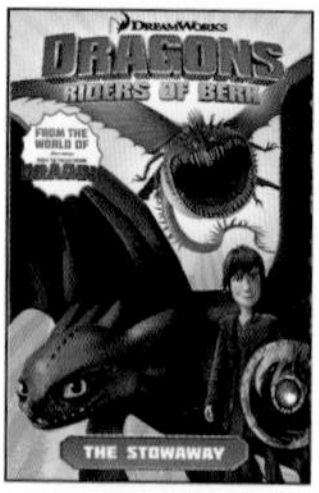
DreamWorks
DRAGONS
RIDERS OF BERK
THE STOWAWAY

DreamWorks Dragons: Riders of Berk – The Stowaway

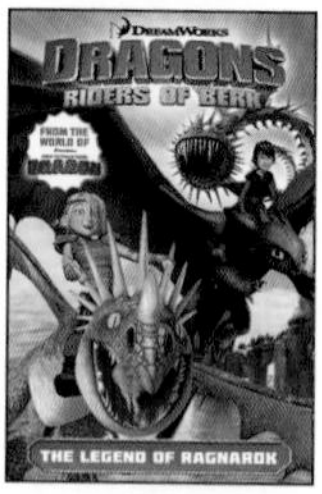
DreamWorks
DRAGONS
RIDERS OF BERK
THE LEGEND OF RAGNAROK

DreamWorks Dragons: Riders of Berk – The Legend of Ragnarok

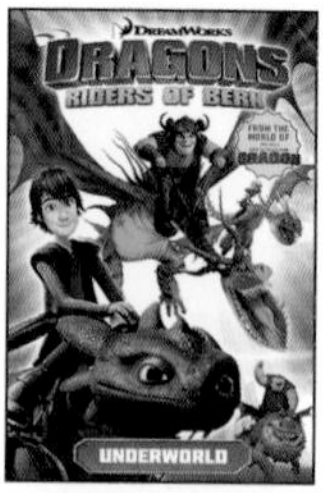
DreamWorks
DRAGONS
RIDERS OF BERK
UNDERWORLD

DreamWorks Dragons: Riders of Berk – Underworld

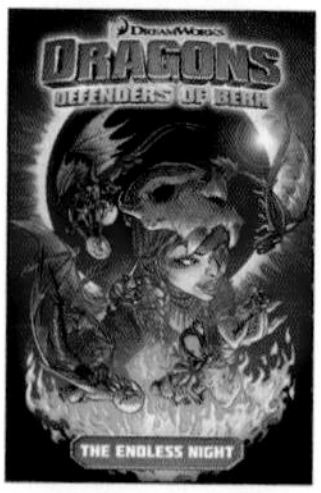
DreamWorks
DRAGONS
DEFENDERS OF BERK
THE ENDLESS NIGHT

DreamWorks Dragons: Defenders of Berk - The Endless Night

WWW.TITAN-COMICS.COM

ALSO AVAILABLE DIGITALLY

TITAN COMICS

DREAMWORKS ANIMATION SKG

TITAN COMICS COMIC BOOKS

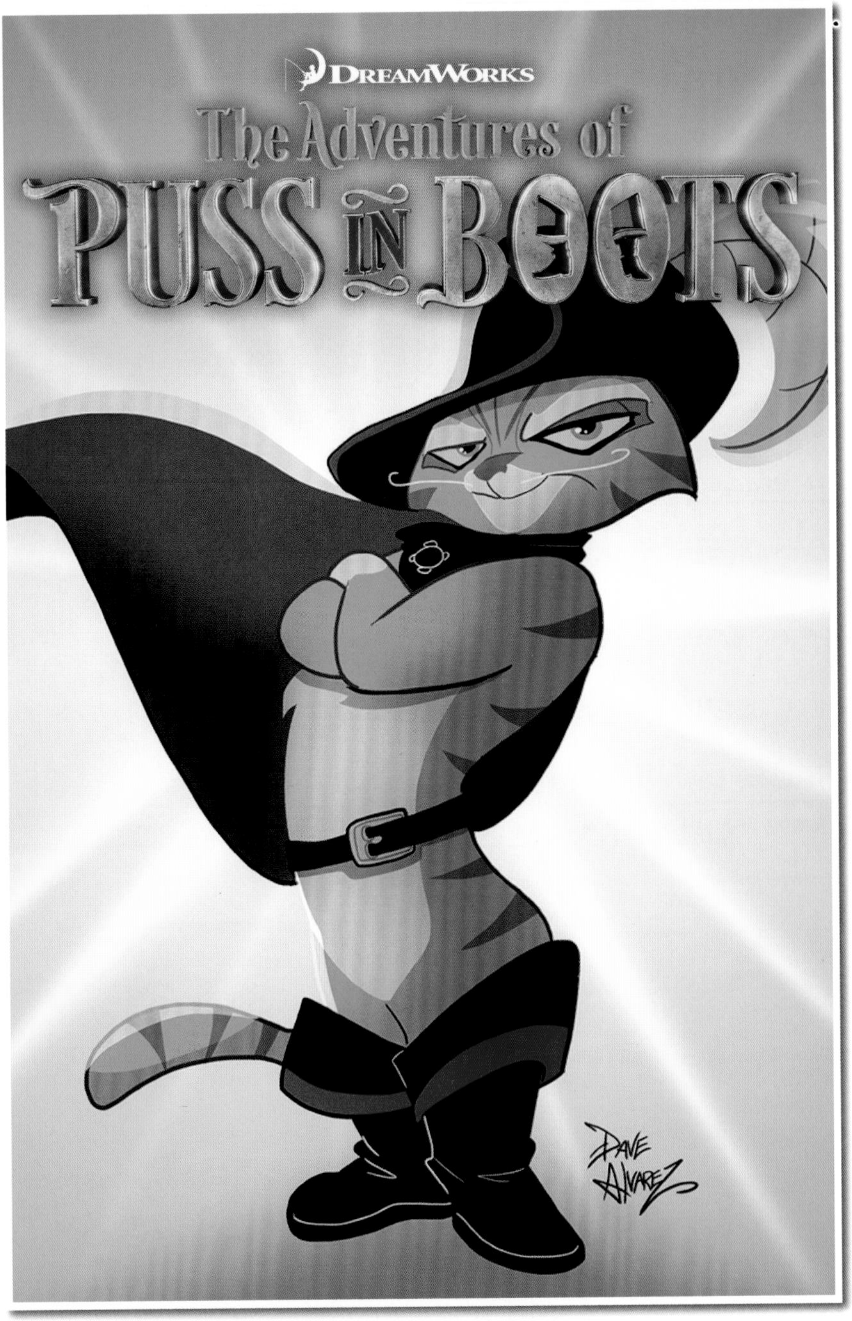
DREAMWORKS
The Adventures of
PUSS IN BOOTS
DAVE ALVAREZ

AVAILABLE MONTHLY NOW!

ALSO AVAILABLE DIGITALLY.

WWW.TITAN-COMICS.COM

TITAN COMICS

DREAMWORKS ANIMATION SKG

TITAN COMICS GRAPHIC NOVELS

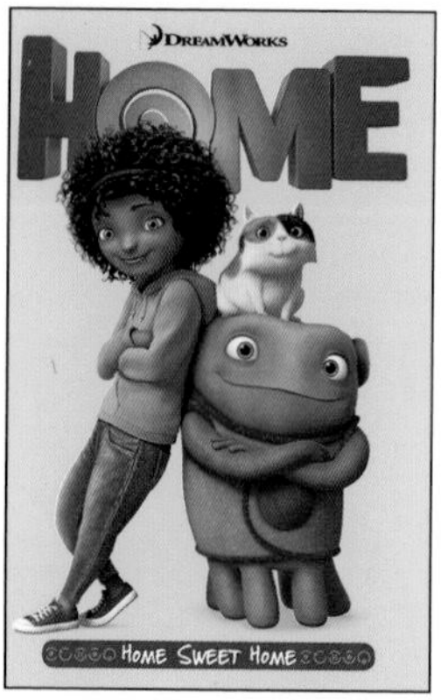
DreamWorks
HOME
Home Sweet Home

HOME: HOME SWEET HOME

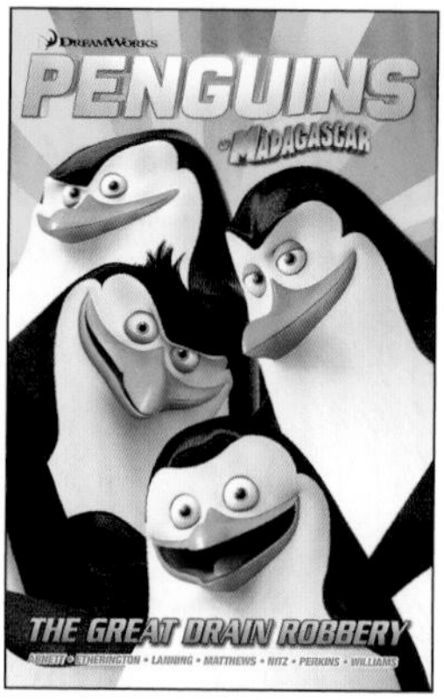
DreamWorks
PENGUINS
of MADAGASCAR
THE GREAT DRAIN ROBBERY

PENGUINS OF MADAGASCAR:
THE GREAT DRAIN ROBBERY

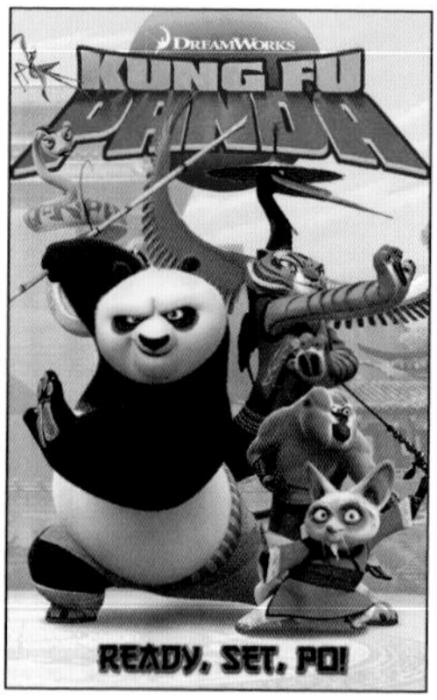
DreamWorks
KUNG FU
PANDA
READY, SET, PO!

KUNG FU PANDA –
READY, SET, PO!

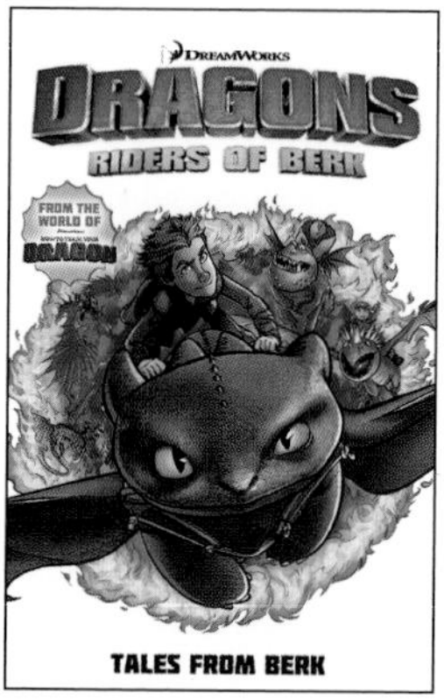
DreamWorks
DRAGONS
RIDERS OF BERK
TALES FROM BERK

DREAMWORKS DRAGONS:
RIDERS OF BERK – TALES FROM BERK

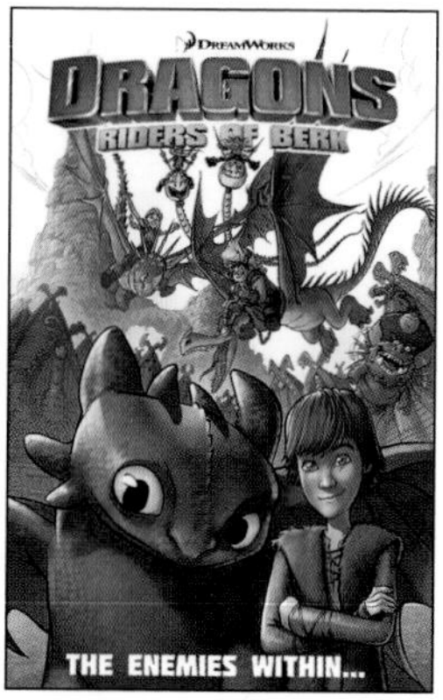
DreamWorks
DRAGONS
RIDERS OF BERK
THE ENEMIES WITHIN...

DREAMWORKS DRAGONS:
RIDERS OF BERK – THE ENEMIES WITHIN

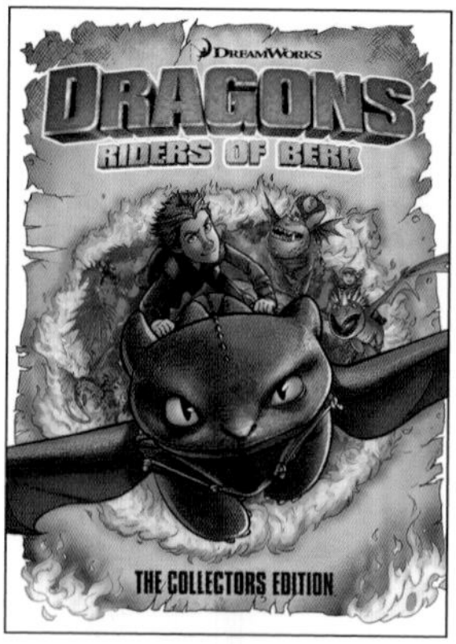
DreamWorks
DRAGONS
RIDERS OF BERK
THE COLLECTORS EDITION

DREAMWORKS DRAGONS: RIDERS OF BERK
COLLECTORS EDITION

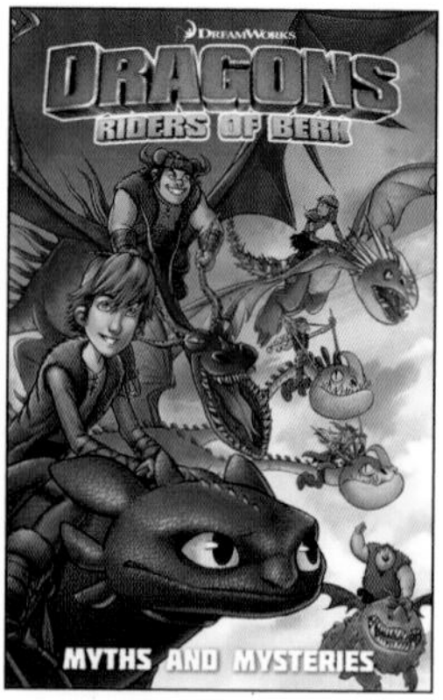
DreamWorks
DRAGONS
RIDERS OF BERK
MYTHS AND MYSTERIES

DREAMWORKS DRAGONS:
MYTHS AND MYSTERIES
COMING SOON

TITAN COMICS

WWW.TITAN-COMICS.COM

DREAMWORKS ANIMATION SKG